Good Thing Bad Thing

A Novel by Nick Alexander

Nick Alexander

Nick Alexander was born in 1964 in the U.K. He has travelled widely and has lived and worked both in the U.K. and the U.S.A. He currently lives with two cats and three goldfish in Nice, France. Nick is the editor of the bi-weekly satirical news site www.BIGfib.com

Good Thing, Bad Thing is his third novel. The first two novels in this series, *50 Reasons to Say Goodbye* and *Sottopassaggio* are also available from BIGfib Books.

For more information, to contact the author, or to order extra copies please visit his website on www.nick-alexander.com

Acknowledgements

Thanks to Fay Weldon and Robert Thicknesse for encouraging me when it most counted.

Thanks to Rosemary and Dave for all their help and encouragement with the manuscript, and to Richard Labonte for his proofing skills. Final thanks go to Hugh Fleetwood for his assistance with the Italian dialogue.

"Things are seldom what they seem,
Skim milk masquerades as cream."

- William S. Gilbert

When Sorry Is The Hardest Word

There are so many good-looking men at Nice airport; I stand and watch as they stream through the stuttering automatic doors – a bizarre male beauty parade.

There are young guys in trendy two-tone sweatshirts, and smooth businessmen in luxurious suits. Dreamily I imagine dating them, imagine being the person waiting for the guy with the bleached highlights, or the high-flying executive with the shiny briefcase – and wonder, *how would that be?*

And now, here he is, the one I'm waiting for. He's hiking his bag over his shoulder and looking around, scanning the room. He hasn't seen me yet – and for a moment I am able to see him dispassionately – just a man in the crowd.

Not the best looking of the bunch, I decide, not the best dressed, nor the most athletic. But there's something about him all the same – an optimistic bounce in his step that makes him look less bored than most of the others, maybe more alive.

And now he sees me, and when our eyes meet we break into matching grins, and that, I realise, is the thing that makes him the special one. The fact that simple eye contact makes us grin so broadly, stupidly even.

He pushes through and drops his bag at my feet. "Jeeze that's heavy," he says.

I laugh. "It's a big old bag. What did you do? Bring a friend?"

Tom smiles and hugs me. As he does so I feel him shrug. "It needs to be big," he says. "A month is a long time."

I heave on the steering wheel and pull out onto the *Promenade Des Anglais*.

"Are you sure you want to head straight off?" I say. "I mean there's no reason at all why we can't go home first, have a cuppa with Jenny, even spend the night there."

Tom shakes his head. "Nah, I like this idea," he says. "Take a bus to get the train to get the plane, and then, hop! We're away. The only thing missing is the Arab man."

I frown at him. "I'm sorry?"

"You can reach me by rail-road," he sings. "Cross the desert with an Arab man..."

"Oh right, yeah," I laugh. "Sometimes your musical references scare me."

"And I'll see Jenny and Sarah when we get back," Tom continues. He raps the dashboard. "So, just drive baby."

I lean over and peer in the side mirror.

"Isn't it hard driving this thing," he asks. "I mean, here, in France?"

I shrug. "It's not the easiest thing," I say. "I'd rather have a left-hand drive... But you get used to it." I click on the indicators and swap lanes then settle back into my seat.

"The worst thing is parking it," I say. "Especially in Nice. It's been a bitch trying to find any spaces big enough."

Tom pulls some chewing gum from the pocket of his denim jacket and offers me a stick. "She's keeping it then?" he asks.

I glance at him briefly and frown. "Oh, Jenny? I really don't know," I say. "She intended to... I mean, that's why she brought it here, but I think now she's driven all across France with it... well she's had enough really."

"Good for us." Tom strokes the door. "I love these old things."

"Yeah," I agree. "Good for us." I smile at Tom and then glance back at the road. "Only don't ever say that to her, will you?"

"Say what?"

"Don't call her beloved van an *old* thing," I laugh. "It may look like a 1960's hippy bus, but it's almost new."

Tom chats to me a while as I drive east into Nice, then out north towards the Autoroute. He tells me about his new job in foreign exchange.

"It's weird really," he says. "My uncle only reappeared on the family scene last month... I don't remember ever having met him before – I mean, I did when I was tiny – and now, suddenly I'll be working for him. Anyway, he's almost doubling my salary," he tells me excitedly.

But I can hear that he's tired, and I'm not surprised at all when I glance across a few minutes later and see his head lolling forwards.

At the Italian border I have to lean across him to grab a ticket from the tollbooth – one of the disadvantages of having a right-hand drive car – and he briefly awakens, giggles and pecks me on the cheek before falling back to sleep.

The Brazilian-built VW drives like a roller coaster, inexorably gathering speed on the downhill runs, and then chugging its way reluctantly through the climbs. It may be nearly new, but it drives like a sixties' original.

The sky is unusually grey for the beginning of June and I worry about the dark tint along the northern skyline, wondering if we're going to get early summer storms. It's amazing how like England just about anywhere can look when you replace azure blue with blanket grey. At least with the van we don't have to sleep in a tent.

As I drive, Tom shifts and stirs as he tries to get comfortable. I'm feeling really happy – all my favourite things are rolled into one: travelling, driving, camping, Italy, Tom... A wave of love – for Tom, for life – sweeps over me, and my vision mists. It's all just *too* perfect.

I stop that thought in its tracks. *"Yes, things can work out,"* I tell myself, *"even if only for a while."*

Tom drags me from my reverie. "I need a piss," he says.

I turn and see him notice the look in my eyes. I see him register right where I am right now. He smiles broadly and winks at me.

"No problem," I say. "I need petrol anyway. This thing drinks more than..." I shrug searching for a comparison.

"Liza?" Tom laughs.

"Liza?"

"Yeah, Liza with a Zee," Tom says.

"Yeah, she'll do," I laugh, "though I hear she's on the wagon now, so that's maybe a bit unfair."

The service station is as Italian as a service station can be, the long standing-only bar filled with a boisterous rabble of Italian lorry drivers jostling for service. Everyone is knocking back microscopic doses of caffeine served by the waist-coated barman.

"Madness," Tom laughs.

I nod. "I'm so glad everything's not the same though," I say. "I love all this."

Tom nods as he looks around. "Yeah," he says. "Give it ten years and this'll be a Little Chef."

"Or a McDonald's," I say, bleakly.

The campsite at Bonassola is a disappointment, but we're both too tired to care. We accept the proffered square of muddy turf set amongst random caravans that look, for the most part, as though they will probably never move again. The guy at the check-in desk is ugly too – a spotty adolescent with a thick top lip and a spluttering lisp.

I put a pan of water on to boil and peer out at the desolation.

"Not a *good* start to the holiday," I say.

Tom rubs my shoulder as he squeezes past. "A night in a camper van, snuggled up with you," he says. "Sounds okay to me."

He starts to fold out the cushions that form the sleeping area. "Anyway, we can always move on tomorrow."

I pull a face. "Erm, *hello?*" I say. "We're *definitely* moving tomorrow!"

We sit on the side step and eat bowls of pasta with tinned tomato sauce, then dump the bowls in the tiny sink and crawl into bed.

"It's actually really comfortable," Tom says, snuggling to my back.

"Mmmm," I agree. "I'm so glad we're doing this."

We listen to the sounds of Bonassola: an Italian TV from the caravan behind us, a main road far away to the left, and the ubiquitous Mediterranean moped buzzing up some distant hill.

As the first wave of sleep drifts over me, I hear someone snoring, and the last thing I realise is that it's me.

I wake up early; the sun has returned and is pushing through the deep orange curtains. Somewhere on-site a baby screams.

I snuggle against Tom and he groans and stretches, then pushes back against me. I move and push my morning hardness against his buttocks and he makes an "um" noise and wriggles still closer. I reach round to touch him but he intercepts my hand with his own and pulls it up around his chest with a mumbled, "Sorry."

The dozing ends suddenly when Tom leaps from the bed and starts pulling on his jogger bottoms. "The time has come to check out the local plumbing," he declares, pulling a face.

I grimace, roll over and watch him leave. "Good luck," I say. "It's grim."

When Tom returns, I look up from the kettle which is just starting to whistle. "God I love all this," I tell him.

"I'm not loving the toilets," he says.

I grin. "No, all *this*," I say sweeping my hand over the mini kitchen. "I can't explain why, but every bit of it, from the smell of the butane gas to the taste of plastic cups. It just all leaves me ecstatic."

"There's something about the sound too," Tom says. "The dull echo in here that makes it sound like camping, you know what I mean?"

I nod and pour the water. "I do," I say.

"It's all a bit girly I guess," Tom says. "Maybe that's why we gay boys like camping so much."

I frown, indicating non-comprehension and fiddle in the tiny drawer for a teaspoon.

"You know, like a wendy-house," he explains. "Play tea-sets and all."

We settle for cornflakes with long-life milk and promise each other that we'll buy proper Italian food just as soon as we can, and then – my favourite bit of all – we close the side door, climb into the front seats, and drive our home right out of there.

Bonassola is a beautiful little town – it turns out to that we missed the centre completely last night. Nestled against the azure sea it's truly tempting, but after a moment's hesitation we drive on through. Tom has his heart set on Cinque Terra, five seaside towns linked by rocky walkways, which his ex, Antonio, told him are amongst Italy's most beautiful tourist spots.

The road swoops and climbs back up into the sumptuous greenery of the vine-covered hills, hills that echo and throw back the spluttering sound of the rear, air-cooled engine.

Zigzagging down the hillsides are networks of seated lawnmower contraptions mounted on flimsy steel monorails. We figure out that they must be the grape harvesting solution in this difficult terrain.

"I'd love to have a go on one of those," I tell Tom.

"Yeah," he laughs. "I wonder how fast they go."

Just after Levanto, I pull over to a siding and we buy ripe, red tomatoes and deep-green lettuce along with the smallest most vibrantly coloured courgettes I have ever seen. While Tom boils eggs and prepares a tuna salad, I sit and peer out through the sliding windows at the glimmering sea. A gentle breeze flutters the roped-back curtains and makes the cooker flame flicker and spit.

Tom leans down and peers out over the rolling blue. "It's a great spot," he laughs. "Can't we just stay here?"

By the time we get to Monterosso, the first of the Cinque Terra towns, it's already gone half-past eight.

"The light will be fading soon," Tom comments glumly. "And it ain't gonna get any easier to find another campsite in the dark. We should have left earlier."

It's true we had a long lunch – I even dozed off in the sun – but the road was unexpectedly slow, a veritable obstacle course of hairpin bends, tractors, mopeds and other, more leisurely camper-vans.

"Oh I expect we have another hour," I say already noisily accelerating back up the hill. "There'll be another campsite soon enough."

"If it's not chock-a-block as well," Tom says.

We're both feeling grumpy and tired. I'm starting to wish we *had* stayed in the car park.

"Yeah, well," I say. "Let's wait and see, eh?"

Tempers finally fray as the last light fades.

"So where are you going *now*?" Tom asks.

I know that it's just run-of-the-mill holiday stress, but Tom's negativity is starting to wind me up.

"Where does it *look* like I'm going?" I retort, pointing at the muddy track in front.

"Okay, let me rephrase that," Tom says. "I can see *where* you're going..." he says. "You're driving me into the middle of a forest. What I *don't* know is *why*."

"Probably to slit your throat," I mutter.

"Sorry?"

"Nothing, look..." I slow to a stop and put the handbrake one. The forest looks eerie and dangerous, the night overpoweringly present.

"Tom," I say, keeping my voice as measured as possible. "We've been driving for *hours... I've* been driving for hours. We've been told that there are three campsites around here, and we've found two, both of which are full. The third one clearly doesn't want to be found, and I'm frankly sick of going up and down looking for the fucking thing. Especially with the love of my life – who is fast turning into Lucifer himself – barking in my ear."

I glance across at him. He does a slow blink, duly admonished. I reckon it's as close as I'll get to an apology tonight.

"So I thought I would just drive along this track here," I continue, "into the middle of the woods and find a spot to sleep. Then we can sort out a better plan in daylight, *okay*?"

Tom sighs and nods.

"Now if you have a *better* plan," I say, "Please, I mean, *per-lease*... take the wheel, and put it into action."

Tom blows through his lips. "Sorry," he says, "it's just... whatever... That's fine."

The "Sorry," calms me, but the "it's just," doesn't. I am about to ask what he means when headlights sweep through the cabin. A vehicle is bumpily heading down the track.

"Shit," I say. "Now I'll have to reverse this fucker all the way..."

I crunch the gears into reverse, but the second we start to move, the car gives us a blue flash and emits the tiniest hint of a wail.

"Oh *great*," Tom says. "*Polizia*."

The policeman who steps from the car is the short, dark, fantasy kind you only really find in Italy. His impeccable Italian police uniform, red-striped trousers-and-all, does nothing to lessen the effect.

"*Hello!*" I mumble as he heads, naturally, to Tom's window.

He rattles off a bout of high-energy triple-speed Italian.

Tom glances at me with raised eyebrows and says, a hint of sarcasm in his voice, "*He* wants to know where you're going *as well*," before turning back to the policeman and starting, hesitantly, to reply.

He's stuttering and stammering and playing up his foreignness, but even so, I only really catch about one word per sentence. The gestures though are clear enough. The policeman is pointing back the way we came.

"He wants the passports," Tom explains, digging into the glove compartment.

The policeman studies my passport briefly then flips it shut and hands it back to Tom. "Mark," he says giving me a nod as he opens Tom's.

"Tom," he reads. "Tom *Gambino.*" His voice rises so noticeably as he says, "Gambino," that I turn back to study his expression.

"*Gambino?*" he repeats. "*Italiano?*"

Tom shakes his head and nods at his passport. "*Inglese*," he says, nodding his head for emphasis.

"*Un momento.*"

The policeman walks to his car, leans in and reaches for the walky-talky.

"What's *that* all about?" I snigger. "Is there something you haven't told me?"

"Don't!" Tom says.

"*Is* it Italian?" I ask. "I never really thought about it."

Tom nods and shrugs. "Yeah, grandparents, well, one of them anyway. Never met him though. He died before I was born, came over in the thirties…"

"I always knew you were exotic," I say.

Tom raps his fingers on the armrest and pulls a face. "Yeah, sure am," he laughs, nervously glancing at the policeman. "Born and bred in Wolverhampton."

When the policeman returns, he rattles off an even longer bout of Italian, hands Tom his passport and winks at him. "*Buona Notte Signor Gambino*," he says, a definite smirk on his face. Then he bangs the side of the van, and spins sharply back towards his car.

"Okay... So he says the third campsite is full..." Tom tells me.

"Shit!"

"But he says there's a farm he knows where we can camp."

My skin prickles with relief. I was actually thinking he might book us for trespassing. "So, you escape the law once again, *Signor Gambino*," I say.

"*Don't!*" Tom admonishes. "There's a siding or something a few meters behind you. He says to reverse into it."

"And then?"

"He says to reverse a bit into the bushes so he can get past and then turn around and follow him. It's not far..."

"Oh," I say, the stress now falling completely away. "Cool."

Tom frowns. "*Yeah*," he says thoughtfully.

"And?"

Tom shrugs. "I'm not quite sure, but I *think* he said he'll tell him..." he pauses and shakes his head.

"Yeah?"

"Sorry, I'm just thinking about the words he used. *Carino*."

"*Carino?*" I repeat.

"Yeah," Tom says dubitatively. "I think it means cute."

"Cute?"

"Yes. I *think* he said he'll tell his friend – the one with the farm – tell him how *cute* we are," Tom says.

"Oh," I say, starting to reverse again. "Was that both of us then, or just me?" I ask with a chuckle.

"Well actually, *I'm* the one he winked at," Tom laughs.

The police car squeezes past, and I turn in the clearing and head back down the track.

"At least we have somewhere to stay. Quite a result, considering..."

"Hum," Tom says mockingly. "What would you do without me? I mean, cute or not, I can't help but wonder how you manage when I'm not around."

"I'm not sure either, Signor Gambino," I say.

Tom is snoring, oblivious to the shifting shadows of the countryside around us, dead to the chilling noises in the distance. I try to resist the urge to peer out through the curtains again – it only makes things worse – but I can't help it. We may have been told to camp here by a friendly cute policeman, but I'm freaked.

The overhanging trees are moving spookily in the cold blue light, casting twisting shadows from the nearly full moon. Every few minutes a metallic scrape breaks the rustling quiet of the forest, followed by a dull thud. I try to imagine what could make such a noise in the country at 2 AM.

A guillotine being raised, and then repeatedly dropped? *"Ridiculous,"* I tell myself.

I snuggle to Tom's back, hoping that he will awaken and reassure me, but he just groans and rolls away, so I prop myself up on my elbows and peer out at the night.

Grate – thud. The guillotine falls again.

It seems that I will never get to sleep.

Tom's arm pulls me towards him until we're as snug as spoons in a drawer. I open one eye and squint at the orange brightness. The air inside the van is stifling. The roof of the van is so hot I can feel the heat radiating from it.

"Hot," I mumble.

Tom reaches behind and slides open one of the small windows letting in a welcome gust of oxygen, and then slithers and snuggles back against me.

"Morning gorgeous," he says. "You sleep okay?"

I laugh. "Not really," I say. "I got spooked about noises outside."

"Noises?" he says with a yawn. "You should have woken me; I slept like a log."

"You slept like a log because I *didn't* wake you," I mumble.

Tom rolls away with a grunt and, worried that I have offended him, I follow his movement and enlace him with my arms.

"Sorry," I say. "Bad night."

Tom shrugs and yawns. "Sunny," he says. "Again!"

I nuzzle the nape of his neck, and reach down for his dick but he pushes my hand away again with a simple, "Nah, not now."

Behind his back, I frown and sigh. "Is something wrong?" I ask.

Tom strains to look back at me. "No," he says. "Why?"

"It's just you didn't want to yesterday either," I point out.

"I was knackered yesterday," he says.

"And today?"

"Today *you're* knackered," he laughs.

I push against him. "Doesn't stop *me* though; *see*?" I say pushing my dick against his buttocks.

Tom nods towards the window. "It just feels a bit public," he says.

I laugh and push him over onto his front then roll my weight onto his back.

"We're in the middle of nowhere," I laugh.

A gust of wind ripples the tiny curtains so I reach up to pull them closed. And freeze. A face is staring back at me, mere inches beyond the window. Piercing green eyes, deeply tanned, maybe even a little dirty – jet-black dishevelled hair, late thirties maybe early forties. Good looking, but wild.

"Jesus!" I say.

Tom looks up. "Jeeze!" he repeats, tugging at a coat to cover himself.

"*Buongiorno*," the man says. He lifts a small carrier bag to the window and waves it at us. "I bring eggs and milk. You English?"

Tom nods. "Yeah, thanks, but…"

"I scare you," he says. "Sorry."

"No," Tom says. "It's okay."

"Sure scared the shit out of *me*!" I mutter.

"And you busy," the man says with a wink. "I understand. Here." He waves the bag at us again.

Tom glances at me and when I shrug, then he reaches out and takes it. "Thanks, sorry… Look, I'll get up," he says.

But the man shakes his head. "No, you have a fat morning," he says. "You travel and tired."

He gives us a little wave, before adding, "You come find me later, you come find Dante." As he says his name he points to himself, then to the right. "In farm."

And then, as though he is in a lift, his face slides downwards and vanishes from the window.

I take the bag and peer inside. "Fuck, he scared me," I say, handing it back to Tom.

"Yeah," he says. "Me too! Fresh eggs for breakfast though."

"So there *shall* be buns for tea," I say in my best posh accent.

Tom frowns at me and I shrug. "Never mind. It's from the *Railway Children*."

"Weird looking bloke though," Tom says.

"Yeah," I agree. "Cave man. Do you think he saw us, I mean…"

"Can't see how he could have missed it really," Tom says, reaching for his jogging bottoms.

"Hey, don't get up," I say, "I haven't finished. I haven't even started actually."

Tom pushes me away playfully and kneels on the bed. "As I was saying," he says. "It's a bit public here."

I step from the van and scan the surroundings; in daylight everything looks stunningly mundane. The headless man is a warped olive-tree trunk; the weird crop circle – nothing more than a flattened area where some farm machinery has stood. The eerie moonlight has been replaced by sunlight dappling the forest floor through vibrant green leaves.

Tom jumps down beside me and rests a hand on my shoulder. "Demons all gone then?" he asks, reading my mind.

I nod. "Looks that way," I say. "Best to move on before they come back though," I add.

"Eggs for breakfast then?" Tom asks with a shrug.

I smile at him. "Yeah, and those dry toasty things," I say. "We've still got some of those."

Tom brews coffee and scrambles eggs, and I fold out two deckchairs and sit and watch the swirling of the long grass in the summer breeze. Behind me the clattering of utensils and the opening and closing of tiny cupboards sounds familiar and reassuring.

"Milk?" I ask as Tom hands me the coffee pot.

He wrinkles his nose. "I wouldn't," he says. "It smells funny…"

"Funny?"

"Yeah," he laughs holding the bottle towards me.

I shake my head. "Nah, it's okay," I say. "I'll take your word for it."

As we walk, I strain to peer over the straggling bushes at the farmhouse beyond. Tom, beside me, is studying the ground.

"You looking for tracks?" I ask.

He kicks a rusty beer can lying in the field and looks up at me. "Uh?"

"You look like you're tracking someone," I say.

Tom shakes his head. "Nah, mushrooms," he says. "It looks like a field where we used to go mushrooming... near Brighton, but I think it's too dry here."

I nod towards the gate. "We just pop in, say goodbye and bugger off, okay?"

Tom shrugs. "Yeah," he says. "I guess so."

"I don't want to get caught looking for a campsite in the dark again," I say.

We push through the rusty gate, which creaks and grates – I realise that this is the noise I heard during the night – and cross the dusty farmyard. Chickens cluck and scatter around us.

Bits of disused farm equipment lie around and just to the left of the front door sits a sofa – it's been covered with a mouldy tarpaulin.

We knock on the weather-beaten front door, and peer through the dirty windows into a functional, but threadbare kitchen – a worn wooden table and unmatched chairs, a black wood-burning range.

"Looks like he lives alone," I say.

"How can you tell?" Tom asks.

I shrug. "Wives don't let places look like that," I say.

"Yeah," Tom agrees thoughtfully. "A bit of a hermit by the looks of it."

We walk the length of the building and peer down the side of the house. It's exactly the same as the front – dusty ground picked dry by the hens, an old lawnmower, a rusty oil-drum, three car tyres piled up...

"Looks like he's gone out," I say, inexplicably relieved. "Maybe we should just leave a note." I check my pockets for a pen.

"And maybe we could leave some cash for the eggs? He doesn't exactly look rich," Tom says.

"Hey," I say, nodding at something on the ground. "Rainbow flag," I say, pointing.

As Tom walks over and lifts one corner of the faded flag, I jerk my head sideways. "Come on Tom," I say. "Lets just go."

Tom nods, and I wonder if he too is relieved that we haven't bumped into the wild-man. We turn to go, but freeze. I hear Tom take a sharp intake of breath.

"Again!" I say, laughing tightly. Dante is standing only a few feet away. He's grinning broadly, madly even. And he's covered in blood.

Tom too laughs nervously. "Oh, *hello*," he says.

Dante nods and wipes his hands on the stained apron but says nothing.

"We came to say goodbye," I tell him.

He shakes his head and continues to smile. "No," he says. "Not goodbye. Not yet."

Dante drags the tarp off the sofa revealing an unlikely leather chesterfield. "You sit," he says, as he goes inside.

"He makes me nervous," I whisper.

"We'll have a coffee and go," Tom says. "Relax."

"*Relax...*" I repeat. "He's too smiley."

Tom snorts discreetly.

"He could be an axe murderer," I whisper. "He's covered in blood."

"It's a farm," Tom laughs, as if this explains everything.

We sit and wait in subdued silence. Occasionally a gust of wind blows the tall grass beyond the fence, and then a few seconds later the dust of the yard swirls in delayed sympathy.

"Our lives are mad really," Tom says after a moment. "I mean, you never really realise it, but there are *loads* of people still living like this."

"Not sure I'd want to though," I say looking around and wrinkling my nose.

Tom wobbles his head from side to side. "Sure, not *exactly* like this. But it would be good to slow it all down sometimes, you know what I mean?"

"Yeah, well, it's certainly slow round here," I say. "It's still about, what, 1950?"

Tom laughs. "Yeah," he says quietly. "It could still be the thirties really."

"*Allora!*"

We turn to see Dante backing through the door. He's carrying a tray with a hexagonal espresso pot and three mismatched cups.

"Breakfast is good?"

I smile. "The eggs. Lovely!" I enthuse.

Dante has changed his top and removed the apron, but his shoes are still bloodstained. He follows my gaze and looks down at his feet. He frowns, then says, "Pigs. I…"

He places the tray at our feet and looks up at us and then makes a slitting action across his throat.

Tom nods. "You *killed* them?"

Dante nods enthusiastically. "Yes, I *kill* them," he says proudly.

He positions a plastic crate opposite the sofa, then sits on it and pours an inch of the thick black coffee into each of the cups. "You don't like pigs?" he says peering up at me from beneath heavy brows, "Jewish?"

"*Jewish?*" I say wrinkling my brow quizzically.

"You don't eat pig?" Dante repeats.

"No," I say. "It's not that… No not that at all… I don't eat *any* meat, neither of us do."

Dante pulls a face and hands me a chipped yellow cup.

"We're vegetarian," Tom explains.

The bitter scent of the coffee reaches my nose. "You have any sugar?" I ask.

Dante shakes his head. "Sugar will kill you," he says. "No sugar."

I nod. "We have some in the van," I say, pointing. "Maybe I should just nip…"

Dante frowns. "No sugar," he repeats.

I force a smile. "I'll just have it without then," I say, casting a nervous glance at Tom.

"So you don't like to kill pig," Dante says.

I shake my head, and wonder if he's ever met a vegetarian before.

"Why?" Dante asks with a shrug.

I shrug back and smile dumbly. "I don't like to kill animals," I say.

Dante nods.

"There are lots of vegetarians in England," Tom says.

Dante nods and sips his coffee.

"So you farm other things, or just pigs?" I ask.

He frowns, and seemingly ignores my attempt at conversation. "So if you are in the forest and you meet... *Come si dice cinghiale?*"

"Wild pig?" Tom volunteers.

Dante nods. "You meet *cinghiale*... So you kill or *cinghiale* kill you?" The question is directed at me.

I shrug again. "It never happened," I retort.

Dante frowns.

"I never had to face wild pig in the forest," I explain.

"We live in the city," Tom adds.

Dante nods knowingly. "But philosophy is about the what *not* happen," he says. "So?"

Tom shrugs and turns to Dante. "If I had to kill it to survive then I would," he says.

Dante nods. "And then you eat? When you have kill it?"

"What is it about meat-eaters?" I think. *"Why are they always so challenged by the presence of a vegetarian?"* I force down another sip of the coffee and wonder if I will really have to drink all of it before we can get away.

"It's not so much the killing," I say. "It's the way it happens, the suffering, the factory farming... That's what I hate."

Dante frowns and looks to Tom for a translation. "Fectory?" he repeats.

"Erm, *allevamento?*" Tom says hesitantly. *"Intensivo?"*

Dante nods knowingly. "So, not..." He sighs in frustration. "Not *la sostanza,*" he says. *"la forma."*

Tom shakes his head indicating that he doesn't understand.

"It's like the French," I say. "Not the substance, but the form... I can't think how to translate it though."

Dante nods and winks. "A very good philosophical point," he says. "Because the *form?*"

We both nod.

"The form, *is* the *sostanza.*"

"The form *is* the substance?" I say adding an almost indistinguishable shrug to show Tom that I only vaguely understand what he means.

Dante tuts and shakes his head then sips his coffee. "So you *never* kill a pig?" he asks.

I smirk at the question and shake my head. "No," I say, wrinkling my nose. "I don't want to either."

"My pigs are very happy," he says.

"*Except* when you kill them," Tom laughs.

Dante frowns.

"Pigs not so happy when you kill them," Tom paraphrases.

Dante squints thoughtfully. *"La forma,"* he says. *"e' molto importante."* He stands, and for a wonderful moment I think that our coffee break is over, that we can stop talking about executing pigs and get out of here.

In fact Dante moves behind the sofa, behind *me*.

"Toma," he says, sliding an arm across my chest.

I stiffen and glance back over my shoulder at Dante who is grinning.

Tom shakes his head. "What exactly…" he says, puzzled; I see him chew his lip, hesitating between amusement and concern.

"Marco is pig," he says.

I see Tom flush red; see the corner of his mouth twitch.

Then Dante leans towards my ear. "I hold like so," he says. "I talk very quiet," he whispers in my ear. "and I scratch eye."

He's actually scratching my ear. I can see Tom is swelling red about to burst, but personally I'm having trouble seeing the funny side of being a demonstration pig. It's just not right.

"Then, when pig is *very* quiet," Dante says.

In a sudden jerky movement he swipes his hand across my throat and stands triumphantly. "Pig is kill," Dante says. "Happy, and kill."

A feeling of outrage starts to sweep over me. Unconsciously I raise a hand to my throat to check I'm not gushing blood, a gesture which sends Tom over the edge. He spasms with repressed laughter. His eyes are sparkling, and starting to tear.

"Form more important than…" Dante says.

I stand. "Erm, *grazie mille*," I say, furiously.

Tom is puce. He opens his mouth but fails to speak and so closes it again.

"I have to go get the van ready," I tell him.

He nods and wipes a tear from his eye. "Five minutes," he gasps. "I'll be over."

"Tom, I don't like him, and it *wasn't* funny," I insist when Tom finally arrives back at the van. I'm feeling particularly pissy about the idea – no doubt imaginary – that they may have been laughing together at my expense.

Tom is still grinning but trying his best to hide it. "I..." he shakes his head and shrugs. "I'm sorry, I can see why..." His voice peters out.

"Why *what*?" I whistle.

"Why you lost your sense of humour," he says. "But you have to admit..." He bites his lip and grins broadly again.

I shake my head. "No Tom," I say. "I don't *have to admit*... And I want to leave now, okay?"

Tom screws up his face and tips his head sideways. "Look, can't we..."

"Why Tom, I mean, what's to do? What's to see? It's a *farm*."

"Just one more night," he whines. "I like it here. I think it's interesting."

I shake my head. "I'm not comfortable. He gives me the creeps."

Tom shrugs. "I quite like him," he says. "I think all that stuff about form and substance is interesting," he says. "He's quite deep."

"There's two of us on this holiday," I point out.

Tom nods. "Exactly," he says.

"And the rainbow flag," I say. "That makes me uncomfortable too."

Tom frowns at me now. "What do you mean?"

I shake my head. "I don't know, but I'm not keen on the fact that he's, well..."

"You don't like him because he's *gay*?" Tom asks, incredulous.

I sigh. "No, it's not that. But for some reason..."

Tom shakes his head. "I don't believe I'm hearing this," he says.

I open my palms. "*What*?"

"That's homophobia..."

"It's noth..."

"It sounds like something Antonio would say," Tom says peevishly. "It really does."

I roll my eyes to the sky. "Look Tom, I'm not homophobic, you *know* that. Come on. This is me here."

Tom shrugs. "So let's stay another night and then leave tomorrow. He's cooking vegetarian *specially*. He said there's even an outside bathroom we can use."

I rub a hand over my eyes. Someone is going to have to give in, and I get the feeling that there it just isn't going to be Tom.

"Oh *Tom…*" I protest.

Inexplicably, Tom takes this to be capitulation on my part. He moves to my side and lays an arm across my shoulders. "Thanks," he says. "It'll be cool. You'll see."

I sigh with the realisation that, though I don't quite understand how, I have just lost. I smile weakly.

"I'm not eating pig though," I say.

Tom smiles. "Ve-ge-tari-an," he says, pedantically.

"And don't let him slit my throat again, okay?"

Tom sniggers. "Promise," he says, adding, "Hey, did I ever tell you how gorgeous you are?"

I smile reluctantly and turn so that he can peck my cheek.

"Oh, and Tom," I say.

He leans back far enough to focus on me. "Yeah?" he asks.

"The philosophical stuff," I say. "All that stuff about *la sostanza* and *la forma…*"

Tom looks puzzled. "Yeah?"

"I worked out the translation."

Tom raises an eyebrow.

"It ain't what you do, it's the way that you do it," I say.

Tom frowns.

"*That's* the English equivalent… It's not the substance but the form that counts… It means, it ain't what you do, it's the way that you do it."

Tom squints at me. "Oh yeah," he says thoughtfully. "I suppose it does."

I nod. "*Deep* huh?"

Dinner with Dante is a surprising affair, a contradictory mixture of understated sophistication and rural minimalism. We eat at a scrubbed kitchen table that could equally be at home in an 1890's inn or a 2006 edition of *Homes and Gardens*. The lighting is low – from a single oil lamp suspended above the table – apparently for aesthetic rather than practical reasons – the house seems otherwise normally wired.

Dante himself has scrubbed up beautifully and in a crisp white shirt he looks stunningly tanned. Only his big calloused hands give away the truth of his earthy lifestyle.

The first course, *"Pomodori all'italiano,"* as Dante describes it, is either the ultimate in less-is-more sophistication, or a minimalist offering from someone who doesn't know how to cook.

He places unmatched white plates in front of us and then serves us each with a single, large, tomato. In a final flourish he adds a sprig of fresh basil to each plate.

As Dante crosses the room to recover his glass, Tom catches my eye, glances down at his plate, and raises an eyebrow.

It's as much as I can do not to laugh – he was telling me only minutes ago how starving he is and a tomato clearly isn't going to do the job.

But once Dante is seated and our glasses have been filled with some *very* earthy Chianti, what a tomato it turns out to be – a perfumed skin stretched over incredibly succulent flesh.

"Wow!" Tom comments. He's apparently as shocked as myself by just how much taste a tomato can have. *"Molto bene!"*

Dante nods and grins broadly. "I not say what I feed plants..." he laughs. "You not like."

I nod. I'm guessing pig-shit or pig-blood and I have neither the need, nor the desire to know more. "Amazing though," I say, forking a thick slice towards my mouth. "They taste like tomatoes we had when I was small."

Tom catches my eye and makes a subtle, slow-down gesture with the flat of his hand. I glance at Dante's plate and see that he is eating very slowly, so I nibble at my slice and try and make it last.

Dante catches something of our secret communication and grins revealing a mouthful of tomato. His eyes sparkle in the lamplight. "Don't worry," he says. "Is more after."

"Good," I say. "Very nice... But very hungry."

Dante smiles back as if this is a good thing to have said, but something about his smile makes me wonder... Something about it strikes me as just a tiny bit forced. I wonder if I am pushing the Pidgin English a little too far.

An awkward silence follows as we try to think of something to say to fill the space while Dante finishes his tomato.

Eventually Tom says, "Oh! Dante, Mark thought of the translation..."

I roll my eyes, embarrassed now at my reduction of Dante's philosophy to a single song-line.

"*La sostanza? La forma...*" Tom explains to Dante, whose brow has furrowed.

"In English," Tom explains, "We say *it ain't what you do it's the way that you do it.*"

Dante nods thoughtfully, and I sigh in relief that he doesn't seem to know the song.

"It is not what you do, it is the way that you do it," Tom expands.

"That what get results," Dante says.

I grit my teeth.

Tom grins broadly. "Hey, you know it!" he exclaims. He turns to me. "He knows it," he repeats.

Dante nods, then points vaguely behind him. "I have radio," he says. "Even in country."

Tom smiles at me contentedly, and I wonder briefly how on earth he can be here with me, in this moment and yet still be so out of touch.

"But it's not the result," Dante says. "Result not *importante...*" He holds his hands parallel in front of him and wrinkles his face as he tries to think how best to explain himself.

Tom and I smile reassuringly and wait.

"Agh!" Dante gasps. "*Frustrante!*"

"*En Italiano?*" Tom prompts.

Dante rattles off a round of Italian and Tom frowns and nods and generally looks engrossed until Dante visibly remembers my presence, and turns to me. "But Mark hungry," he says, standing. "You eat fast," he adds. "Bad for..." He rubs his stomach.

"Digestion," I fill in. "I know."

"Dante's saying that it's not the results that count," Tom explains, "but the things that happen around it, you know, while you're moving towards the result."

"It's not the destination that counts but the voyage?" I ask, again regretting my one-line reduction.

Tom squints and considers my statement. "Maybe," he says. "Something like that anyway."

The next course is as simple as the first – steamed leeks. Or rather steamed leek – one each. Dante drops them onto our plates and then sprinkles them with chopped boiled egg. He hands us a bottle of cloudy olive oil.

Simple food, except that, again, no leek has ever tasted quite like it. "I shake my head in wonder. "This is beautiful Dante," I tell him. "Truly incredible."

He nods. "My garden," he says, pointing at the leeks. "My chicken," he says pointing at the egg. Then he taps the bottle of olive oil and points vaguely over his shoulder. "Old lady," he explains.

"Low mileage food," I say, then realising that there's no way Dante will understand that, I add, "There's a movement, a lot of people, who try to buy local food."

Dante blinks slowly.

"Instead of leeks from Spain, tomatoes from Israel," Tom explains. "People try and buy local food."

Dante nods thoughtfully and contemplates this. "So it ain't what you do," he says, breaking into a broad grin at his own cleverness. "Is the way you do it."

I grin and sip at the wine. Suddenly it seems that the evening has loosened up.

"Modern food," Dante says. "Is like city life."

I peer at him over my glass and then glance at Tom.

"Everything now," Dante says. "Modern food is everything on one plate – city life is everything *now*." He points at the table. "But one thing, one good thing, and then next good thing," he says, making a chopping motion with his hand. "Is better. You see?"

Tom and I meander back towards the van. The wind has gone and it's a balmy summer evening.

"Amazing veg," I say. "And the wine grew on me too…"

"Wasn't so keen on the cheese," Tom says.

I snort at the memory – watching Tom trying to force down Dante's smelly version of cottage cheese was the funniest part of the evening.

"But he's right," I say. "It is great to eat one thing at a time like that."

"Yeah, he's incredible really," Tom says.

I glance at him sideways and frown suspiciously.

"Don't you think?" he adds.

I raise an eyebrow comically.

"His *ideas* I mean!" Tom laughs.

I nod exaggeratedly. "He's cute too though," I say. "Don't you think?"

Tom looks away and kicks randomly at the grass. "He's okay I guess," he says, "but you have to admit, ideas-wise, he's kind of a one-off."

I shrug. "He's interesting for a country boy," I say. "But you know, none of it's exactly earth shattering, not as far as I could understand anyway."

"That's my fault really," Tom says. "I couldn't always keep up, what with listening and translating and everything."

"I got most of it," I say.

"Yeah, I suppose," Tom says. "I thought it was really interesting when he was saying all that stuff about, you know, how when something bad happens... And you never really know whether it's good or bad because of all the causes and effects..."

"The ricochets," I say. "The ripples."

Tom nods. "Yeah." He pauses unexpectedly in front of the van. "Stay up with me a bit?" he asks. "I'm really buzzing tonight."

I nod. "Sure," I say, pulling the two deck chairs together. "It's the coffee I guess. That and the full moon."

Tom looks up at the clear night sky. "It *is* nearly full too," he says.

"It's so dark here," I comment, sitting down and looking up at the sky. "No streetlights, so you can see all the stars."

Tom flops into the chair beside me. "So he was saying," he tells me, "that suppose the car won't start, and you think that's a *bad* thing, because, say, you need to go somewhere urgently."

I turn sideways and lay my legs across his lap. "But maybe you were going to crash," I say. "So *really* it's a good thing."

Tom nods gently.

"See, I *did* understand. It's like that kids' game – *Good Thing Bad Thing*," I say. "Did you never play that?"

Tom frowns. "Good Thing Bad Thing?" he says.

"Yeah," I say. "You take it in turns to tell a story. Say I start with, *Mr B was walking down the street and a bad thing happened – he tripped over.*" Tom frowns so I continue, "And then *you* say, *but a good thing happened because lying there on the floor he saw a ten pound note someone had dropped,* and then *I* say…"

Tom nods in comprehension. "Right," he interrupts. "*Exactly*. But what Dante was saying is that that's why the *process*, the *way* you do things is so important… Because all the ricochets, the ripples, come not from *what* you do but from the way you do it."

I lay my head against the canvas of the deck chair. It is cool and slightly damp. I look at Tom's excited face. It's a while since I saw him this animated, in fact, I'm not sure I have *ever* seen him like this.

"*Wine, full moon, coffee…*" I think.

"It's like the local food thing," Tom continues. "You can eat a leek from the garden, or a leek from, say, Spain, and one will destroy the environment with transport and pollution…"

I smile and close my eyes, but the image of Tom's face remains in my mind's eye. He looks about twenty years old. His voice bubbles on like a brook in springtime. I wonder if he'll get to sleep at all tonight. I wonder if I'll get a cuddle.

"And so some things are *intrinsically* better," he's saying. "and without reasoning, or even counting air miles, Dante was saying that we have a built in ability to *just know* what's good and what's bad. That's why the garden leeks taste better… It's you tasting that they *are* better…"

I try to say, *"That's why I try and buy local veg,"* but I realise that the comment isn't pitched at the right level, so in my half-sleep I merely make a mumbling noise instead.

Tom doesn't pause for a second. "And that, really," he says, "is the main point Dante was trying to make…"

Tom is first up in the morning, and I lie with a pillow over my head, trying to block out the noise of him going through the cupboards. He returns to the bed a little later with Alka-Seltzer and two glasses of water.

"You too then?" I murmur peering up at him.

He winces and nods, and hands me a glass. "That wine was well rough," he says holding out a blue sachet.

I shake my head. "You mix it for me?"

We swallow the bitter mixture and cuddle up, front to back. I rub my nose against his shoulders and drift back to sleep.

It's nearly twelve when we wake up again, and though I'm still feeling a bit worse for wear, my headache at least has gone.

I snuggle against Tom, and again, almost expectedly this time, he prises himself free and sits on the side of the bed where he begins to dress.

I move across the bed, and reach out to stroke his back. "Tom?" I say. "What's wrong?"

He yawns theatrically and looks at me with exaggerated bleariness. "Wrong?" he asks.

I nod. "Yeah," I say, deciding to go straight to the point. "Why aren't we having any sex?"

"I've got a hangover," Tom says. "I thought you had too."

He stands and pulls a sweatshirt over his head, then reaches for the door handle. "I'm going to brave the cold shower I think," he tells me.

"Tom, can you just... *Tom!*"

He glances back at me. "What?"

"I'm *talking* to you," I say.

Tom shakes his head. "You sound like my mother," he says, pushing out into the daylight.

I roll onto my back and sigh unhappily. Now I feel angry as well as hung-over.

I wait miserably for him to return, until eventually, driven by hunger and the desire for coffee, I give up and fold the bed away. Tom is nowhere to be seen, so I set the table for breakfast at the edge of the trees. I save half of the coffee in the pot for Tom, but when it is merely lukewarm I give up and drink it myself.

The day is almost identical to yesterday – clear blue sky, bright white sunlight that seems to bleach the colour out of everything, and a gentle breeze rustling the tall dry grasses.

I eat dry toast from the packet with some marmalade – the butter has been left out and looks rancid – and open a copy of *Gay Times* Tom brought with him.

I flick through until I get to a quiz – "How faithful is your lover?" I stare at it and sigh. It would be stupid to deny that there is some attraction between Tom and Dante, it's plain to see. Hell, even I think Dante is cute, physically... But surely I'm being paranoid?

I peer over at the farmhouse. Tom has gone over to use Dante's cold shower. It would be normal courtesy for Dante to offer him the use of the heated indoor one...

I sigh and stand to see if I can spot Tom, but it is Dante I see, weaving through the field towards me. I groan at the sight. He's wearing tattered khaki shorts, a camouflaged armless flak jacket, and muddy boots. As he nears, he waves a plastic bag at me.

"I bring bread," he says. "Tom says you have not, but he forget to take..."

"Tom?" I say. "Is he..."

Dante shakes his head. "Last night, he tell me... *Told* me," he corrects himself.

I sigh with relief or disappointment, I'm not sure which, and take the bag that Dante has proffered. "Thanks," I say, "but it's okay actually. We have these." I point to the packet of *Biscottes*.

Dante rests a hand on the back of the other chair. "Yes, but fresh is better," he says. "Can I sit?" he asks, nodding down at the chair.

I realise that I'm on the verge of rudeness, so I force a smile and say, "Sure! Please."

I flip the magazine closed and cringe at the semi-naked model on the cover and the red *GAY TIMES* emblazoned across the top.

"And Toma?" Dante asks.

I shrug and wave a hand vaguely across the horizon. "Exploring," I say.

"I think he like the country," Dante says.

I nod. "We both do," I tell him.

Dante disinterestedly pulls the magazine towards him, reads the title, and absentmindedly pushes it away.

"I think you are more city boy," Dante laughs. "Music and lights," he adds, wiggling his fingers across an imaginary skyline.

I'm slightly offended by the judgement. "Music's good," I say. "Lights are useful too," I add.

Dante smiles and nods.

"But trees too," I say looking around.

"The city is *attraente*," he says. "Pulls you, but has no *qualità*."

"No quality?" I frown.

Dante nods.

"If you say so," I say, rubbing a hand across my forehead. I still feel tired, not to mention concerned, angry and a whole load of other things... Mainly I don't feel like having a philosophical debate with Dante.

"You don't agree?" Dante says. "That there is no quality in city?"

"*I don't care,*" I think, but that would be too rude. "Quality means many things," I say. "That's all."

Dante frowns.

"Like quality of life," I point around me. "And quality of experience."

Dante nods.

"But a Mercedes Benz, or a BMW is a quality *car*," I say. "And I don't think that's what you mean. And if you want a quality hifi that makes beautiful music then the city is the best place to find one."

Dante nods thoughtfully. I wonder if I can maybe just pretend to doze off and he'll go away.

"People think quality is *isolamento*," he says.

"Isolation?" I ask, regretting almost instantly that I have further engaged in the conversation.

Dante nods. "From life, yes," he says. "Spend more, on your BMW, never hot, never cold, air conditioning, you know? Never uncomfortable..." He raises a hand to his ear. "Not even hear world outside..."

I nod.

"But hot, cold, tired, noisy... This is *life*," he says.

"Yeah, I see what you're saying," I say vaguely.

"This is luxury. But not *quality*," Dante tells me. "Experience is life, and experience is quality, not *l'isolamento* from life."

I frown and nod. "Look, Dante," I say, pulling a dumb face. "I had too much wine last night you know, and…"

But Dante has understood. "Sorry," he says. "I talk and talk… Too much time on my own."

I nod. "It's okay," I tell him, "it's just…" I tap my head to explain.

Dante smiles and stands. "Sorry," he says. "I go now; I only bring bread."

"Thanks," I say.

But Dante is already heading away across the field. He has his head down, and I actually feel a little sorry for him.

I try to read *Gay Times,* but it's impossible – I just can't concentrate. I read and re-read, but every time I get halfway down the page I realise that though my eyes are skimming the words, my brain is elsewhere.

I'm worrying about Tom; wondering what is happening between us; I'm being relieved that at least he isn't with Dante and realising that now I've sent Dante away, I've made it perfectly possible that he *is* with him…

I decide that that's a stupid thought, and dismiss it, but I carry on thinking it anyway.

We really need to get out of here, I decide. Things seem weird since we arrived here, and there are plenty of good reasons why we need to move on, other than my own illogical jealousy. Places to see, things to buy… Man cannot, after all, live on bread alone.

I fold the bed back out and lie inside the van in an attempt to get some more sleep, but I feel restless and tired, fidgety and uncomfortable, so I get back up and sit in a deck chair outside. Still unable to settle, I stand and pace around the van.

Finally I mutter, "Damn you Tom," and head off around the field.

Walking provides a measure of relief from the darker machinations of my mind. I see some seagulls perched on a branch, and remember with some surprise that we are less than half an hour from the coast.

This in turn, reminds me that this isn't some obstacle course to be endured; we're on *holiday*. We really have to "pull up sticks," drive to the coast, have a swim and a nice meal and get back into the idea of having some fun.

It feels as if we have been here for weeks, not twenty-four hours. It seems as if we are getting entangled in some web and though I can't explain quite what's happening, I know it's not good.

At the far end of the field, beyond the fence that delineates Dante's land is the start of a dense pine forest. It looks carefully planted, managed – man-made.

From a mound on the far end of Dante's land – an old compost heap long since turned to earth – I hurdle the fence and head into the tall trees.

The ground is a soft carpet of pine needles, the air fragrant and cool. There's no birdsong in here, no sound of insect or animal life... It's a peculiar place, here in the dim light of these rows of trees.

I peer up at the tiny patches of sunlight filtering down the trunks and remember last night looking drunkenly at the stars with Tom. At the mere thought of him my heart misses a beat.

"*I'm losing him,*" I think, crazily. I never expected this relationship to last forever – I'm too old and far too cynical for that – but could things really be falling apart on our *first* holiday together.

The hangover, I realise, has left me raw and emotional. I swallow hard and turn back toward the light, determined to leave the forest and these paranoid thoughts behind.

With a lack of grace that would be embarrassing were anyone watching, I scramble back over the fence. It's much harder with the mound on Dante's side of the barrier.

I continue my way along the perimeter, seeing neither Tom, nor Dante; circling the farmhouse in the distance, passing the rusty gate again, and finally ending up back at the van. I slump into a deck chair and reach for the coffee pot to see if there are any dregs, but it's empty.

"That's a loud sigh," Tom says.

My heart skips a beat. The coffee pot almost slips from my hand such is my surprise. "You made me jump!" I say, turning to see Tom's face framed in the window of the VW.

He smiles weakly. "So I see," he says.

I stand and lean into the van. "Have a good walk?" I ask, climbing in and sitting on the end of the bed opposite him.

Tom nods. "Just thinking about stuff," he says. "I bumped into Dante on the way back. He asked if we could help him put up some netting or something tomorrow. It's for the chickens."

"*Oh*," I say, my irritation palpable. "He was over here earlier and he didn't mention it at all."

Tom nods and shrugs. "I said yeah," he says. "Seems the least we can do, after all his hospitality."

"But I..." I start to say. I hesitate, wondering momentarily if forcing our departure is going to be a solution or merely cause for another row.

"We need to talk, you know," Tom says ominously.

I swallow. "I guessed as much," I say, forcing a feeble smile.

"You remember this morning?" Tom asks.

I grunt. "Well of course," I say. Then, softening my tone I add, "I remember."

"You know how I didn't want to..." Tom says, glancing away towards the farmhouse.

It seems suddenly that I have been here before. I'm certain that what is to come is going to be bizarre and inexplicable. And it's going to be terminal.

The possibilities flash through my mind. Maybe he's met someone else; maybe he's cheated on me. Maybe he's going to tell me that he doesn't love me anymore, that for some reason that he *just can't explain*, he doesn't feel the same... Maybe, he's in love with Dante. Stranger things have happened. Stranger things have happened *to me*.

I think I might vomit, a mixture of the hangover and stress I suppose – the stress of remembering just how fragile everything is.

"But I already know that lesson," I think bitterly. *"I don't need to learn it again."*

I look at the back of Tom's head, at the nape of his neck.

When he looks back at me his features soften. "Oh, I'm sorry," he says, with a tenderness that strikes me as incongruous, hypocritical, guilty maybe.

He moves across the bed and tries to place a hand on my leg, but I pull away.

"Please, just say it," I say. "Whatever it is."

He sits back on his heels and frowns. "It's hard," he says.

I nod.

"It's kind of embarrassing."

I wrinkle my brow.

Tom sighs and then blows through his lips. I close my eyes and pinch the bridge of my nose. If he doesn't say whatever's on his mind soon, I will scream.

"Tom!" I say. I hold my breath and listen to the empty silence of the van, to Tom's breathing, to a screeching crow in the distance. The length of the pause strikes me as a bad omen.

"I've got herpes," Tom says.

I breathe. My hand slips to my mouth.

"I'm really sorry," he says. "I should have told you before, only..."

I'm frozen. It's *so* not what I expected him to say.

"It doesn't happen much nowadays, but it flared up really badly..." He pulls a face as if the pain of admitting this is excruciating.

I'm trying to restrain the beginnings of a smirk.

"It started the day I came actually... My dick is like *raw*," he says. "And of course, I've got no fucking *Zovirax* with me."

My eyes are still watering, but I'm grinning broadly now; I just can't help it.

Tom looks at me uncomprehendingly. "Well, don't look so happy about it," he says.

Ve lie side by side. I have one arm behind his head and am stroking the downy hair of his chest.

I don't tell him my paranoid imaginings. I just say that I thought I'd upset him in some way. I know that's dishonest, but now is a good moment, and I don't want to spoil it. Good moments have been few and far between recently.

The true reason for Tom's lack of sexual prowess and his embarrassed reticence to tell me about it... Well it all strikes me as so lovably human, a wave of tenderness sweeps over me for the gorgeous treasure that is a lover; that is this other human being, here, now, just for me.

"You know, we should talk before," Tom tells me.

"Before?" I ask.

"I mean before anyone gets all paranoid and upset."

I nod.

"Dante was going on earlier about how all human conflict comes down to lack of communication."

"So he did talk to Dante," I think.

"He was saying that if everyone would just pause and explain themselves at the very beginning of that moment when you, feel, you know, *againstness*..."

"Mmm," I say, stroking his hair.

"He says that all human conflict comes down to misunderstanding, or paranoid imagination about what other people are thinking... paranoia about their motivations."

I snort gently at the accuracy of the remark, but when Tom looks at me questioningly, I say, "I'm not sure that *all* human conflict comes down to that..."

Tom shrugs.

"I mean, take the Second World War for instance; it wasn't a lack of *understanding*. It was about stopping someone's ambition to rule the world and kill anyone who he didn't like."

Tom tips his head and looks up at me. "You always have a counter-argument, don't you?" he says.

I shrug. "Well, no amount of sitting down and chatting would have convinced Hitler that the Jews or the gays or the disabled were, you know, okay *really*..." I say.

Tom laughs. "I like that about you, you know, the fact that you always see the other side..."

I shrug. "I don't like totalitarianism I guess," I say. "Whether it's Hitler's or a hippy's. The truth always lies somewhere in between; it's always more complex."

But as I say it I feel vaguely fraudulent. I wonder if it isn't simply that I don't like Dante very much, that I just can't resist finding fault in his outrageously accurate perception of our situation.

Tom yawns and moves his head side to side rubbing it against my arm. I reach across and stroke his nipple.

"He's got a theory for everything that Dante," I say. "He was going on to me about..." I close my eyes and try to remember. "Yeah, that's it, *quality*... He was saying people get quality and luxury confused... something like that anyway."

Tom frowns and I shrug. "I was only half listening really," I say. "I was worrying about you."

"Quality and luxury?" Tom says thoughtfully.

"You should ask him about it," I say. "He'd like that."

Tom looks up at me again and smiles. "You changing your mind a bit about Dante?" he asks.

I shrug. "He's okay really," I say, forcing myself to be generous, or is it just to *sound* generous? "He's quite interesting I suppose."

"But you don't really like him," Tom says.

I shrug again. "Nah, not really. He's a bit full on," I say. "Maybe a bit too evangelical for my liking."

Tom nods and looks sideways towards the farmhouse. "I can understand that," he says. "I quite like it though, it makes me feel like I'm young and at college again, you know?"

"Working out the world," I say.

Tom laughs. "Did you do that too? All that sitting up till 5 AM arguing about why we're here?"

I snort. "Yeah; never worked it out though," I say.

Tom pauses for a moment. "Maybe just for this," he says, snuggling closer against me.

"Maybe," I say, leaning over and kissing him. "It's a good philosophy," I add.

"And you don't mind about tomorrow," Tom says. "Helping Dante with the chickens."

I shake my head. "Nah, but let's go out tonight eh?" I say. "Lets go find a restaurant somewhere. I want to feel like I'm on holiday."

Tom rubs his eye. "Yeah, that'd be good. If there is one."

"The seaside's not that far away," I tell him. "There's bound to be restaurants."

"Hmm," Tom says happily. "A real Italian pizza. I'll go over later and ask Dante if he's free."

"Tom," I say. "I thought, you know... Well, I thought we could make it just me and you?"

Tom smiles and sighs. "Sorry," he says. "Sure. I'll go over and let him know. Just so he doesn't think we're having dinner with him."

We have to pay five Euros just to park the van. The weekend crowds in Vernazza are stunning. The swelling crowds of tourists are an assault on the senses, especially after the calm of Dante's field.

"I'm not so sure about this," I tell Tom as a fat English woman barges into my right arm.

"I know!" he says. "Still, now we're here..."

We push our way through the meandering streets down towards the harbour.

"It's a bit like Santorini somehow," Tom comments. "In Greece."

"Except pink instead of white," I say.

"You've been there too?" he asks.

I nod. "Twice," I say. "Loved it."

In the harbour, fishing boats are bobbing up and down on the gentle swell and four or five groups of tourists are simultaneously posing for photos on the quayside.

I nod to a hill on the right. "Shall we try that way?" I say.

Tom grabs my hand and pulls me through the crowd. I'm surprised at the gesture, as he's not usually a one for public handholding, but I think, *What the hell.* There's something about the mad tourist anonymity of the place that makes me just not care.

It's quieter up here – we only occasionally bump into tourists coming the other way – so we press on, zigzagging through the tiny side streets, working our way out toward the edges of the tiny village.

We cross a small *piazza* dominated by a huge candy striped church. Tom nods at two wrinkled black-clad widows sitting on a wall. "Even more like Santorini," he says.

"A note of authenticity," I comment.

"They're probably paid to sit there by the local tourist board," Tom giggles.

Eventually we reach a walkway heading away from the town along the cliffs.

"Do you think this goes all the way to the next town?" I ask.

Tom shrugs. "Maybe..." he says. "Maybe we should see how far it is, look it up in the tourist guide. We could come down and walk it one day."

After a few minutes we quit the path and scramble down to a niche Tom has spotted in the cliff-face. Squeezed into the natural alcove we look down on the distant port, increasingly orange in the fading daylight. We're out of sight from the path above us and people at the restaurants dotted around the harbour are mere dots below.

"Great spot *signor*," I say.

Tom slips an arm around me. "Yeah," he says. "*Waaay* too many people down there." He turns to me and smiles and pecks me on the cheek.

"Hey, I'm sorry I scared you," he says. "I didn't mean to."

I shrug. "It happens," I say. "I'm quite good at scaring myself without anyone's help," I add.

"I know," Tom agrees.

I frown at him and wonder how much he has realised, how much he knows about just how scared I was. I run the hem of his beige shorts between my finger and thumb, and then gently caress his thigh. My stomach rumbles.

"That hungry huh?" Tom laughs.

I snort. "Not hungry enough to face that lot though," I say, nodding at the harbour.

Tom wrinkles his nose. "Do you think we could..."

"Get a *takeaway*?" I say, finishing his phrase.

"We could eat it halfway back," Tom says. "Find a nice spot like yesterday. I saw a pizza place up by the car-park..."

"That's exactly what I was thinking," I say breaking into a grin.

"What?" Tom asks.

"It's just…" I say with a shrug. "Oh I don't know…"

Tom frowns bemusedly, so I continue.

"Well, we're *so* compatible you know."

Tom smiles. "Yeah," he says. "Imagine being with someone who wanted to go to a swanky restaurant every night," he says.

"Oh honey, *perlease* can we go to one of those adorable lil' ole restaurants?" I say, jumping up and pulling Tom to his feet. "Come on, my little soul-mate," I say. "It's pizza in a car-park for you."

Tom smiles at me. "Great isn't it?" he says.

"Hey, look," Tom says, gently nudging me as he looks over at the farmhouse.

I ease off the accelerator and tear my eyes from the pool of light in front of the van. "Huh," I say. "Police car."

"Shit this thing's a bitch to drive," I add as we lurch into a tractor rut. "I swear it drags you magnetically into the holes."

Tom snorts. "The van's fault then," he says.

I raise an eyebrow and sigh. "I haven't seen you fighting to take the wheel," I tell him.

"Yeah, sorry about that," he says, squeezing my leg. "It's just, well, what with it being Jenny's and all."

"Jenny wouldn't mind."

"Yeah, but she's still more your friend than mine," Tom says. "If someone's going to break an axle on a farm track then I'd rather it was you."

I pull up behind the two deckchairs and heave on the hand brake. "Thanks!" I say. "Anyway, we're home. Actually, I suppose you're *always* home in one of these things."

"Home is where your deckchair is," Tom says.

"You're on bed-folding duty," I tell him. "I need a crap."

As I slide the door shut, Tom giggles and says, "Good luck."

He knows how I hate Dante's outside loo.

By the time I return Tom is propped up on pillows. He's reading the *Rough Guide to Italy* in the dim light.

"There's mozzies tonight," he says.

I pull a face. "Oh no! I *hate* that," I say. "Though I'm surprised we haven't had any before really... all those ditches around this field."

As I reach inside the cupboard for the insect spray, Tom tuts. I shrug and wave the can at him. "You *tutting* at me, sweetness?"

He wrinkles his nose. "Just wait and see, okay?" he says. "I hate sleeping in a load of insecticide for nothing."

I shrug again and put the can down beside the bed. "Well, last chance for the fuckers to evacuate," I say. "Cos I'm not doing that bzzzzz bzzzzzzzz comedy sketch all night."

I undress and dump my clothes on the driver's seat, and then I crawl in beside Tom. It's warmer tonight and he has already kicked the sleeping bag down to the end of the bed.

"So what are you reading about, little research assistant?" I ask him.

"Oh, just those walkways," he says snapping the book shut. "How were the sanitary facilities?" he grins.

I pull a face. "I hate that half door affair," I say, "It makes me feel like I'm at school." Tom finds my discomfort so amusing, I add, "It makes me afraid to fart as well."

Tom snorts. "I don't think anyone can hear you in there," he says. "It's miles away from the house..."

"Well, I could hear *them*," I say, "They're talking inside the house."

Tom reaches behind him and clicks off the light. "Yeah?" he says. "Weird, I mean, the outside loo is behind all the sheds and stuff."

I shrug. "Must carry through the pipes or something..." I say.

"Hmm, so what were Dante and the cutey policeman up to?"

I yawn and cuddle up to him. "I could only hear vague voices," I say. "I couldn't hear what they were saying. Mr fantasy man!"

Tom leans over and pecks me on the lips, and then rolls away. "I just love a man in uniform," he says.

"Anyway, if I *had* heard it would have been in Italian."

Tom smiles. "Does fucking *sound* different in Italian then?"

I shrug. "You're the one with an Italian ex," I say.

Tom's smile fades. "Don't," he says.

I squeeze my arm around him. "That was really nice today," I say.

44

"Yeah, despite the bad start," he replies. "But that was a great spot we found on the way home."

"Mmm," I agree. "Lovely view."

"Shit pizza though," Tom laughs.

I grin at the memory. "Soggy pizza," I say. "In Italy. Who would have thought?"

We lie listening to the sounds of the night. I hear Tom's breath start to slow, and note my hard-on starting to fade. Then, just before sleep takes over, I remember something. "There were *three* voices," I say.

But Tom's already asleep.

"How wonderful," I think, jealously. *"To have instant sleep like that."*

I squint out at the darkened interior of the van. All is as it should be, and yet... well, *something* woke me.

I can hear Tom's breathing, the gentle white noise of the trees moving in the breeze, the creak of the rusty gate... There! The buzz of that damned mosquito.

I roll onto my back and hold my breath as I try to work out exactly where the beast is, and slowly, as silently as possible I reach down beside the bed for the can of insect spray.

But as I finger the can, I notice a different noise – a vague, almost inaudible grunt. I turn a little towards Tom, guessing this is some new night-time breathing sound he's added to his repertoire, but no, the noise repeats again and it's coming from outside, from some way away.

I listen hard and identify a different sound, a faint burst of white-noise, like a short gust of wind through a cracked window, or maybe a fly swat, or a skipping rope or... It's followed by the grunt again, low, restrained, muffled.

"Tom," I whisper. "Are you awake?"

"Yeah," he replies immediately, rolling onto his back.

"Can you hear that noise?"

"Yeah, I authorise a chemical attack," he says.

"*Eh?*" I say, wondering if he's still dreaming.

"Go for it," he says, sounding more awake. "If it's bugging you then kill the fucker."

I nudge him. "No, not the mosquito. *Listen*," I say, lifting myself onto my elbows.

I hold my breath again and Tom does the same. A second later the noise repeats – a faint whoosh followed by a muffled groan. Tom sits up beside me, alert and straining to hear.

"It sounds like..." I say, but Tom raises a hand to stop me.

The sound repeats – exactly the same sequence as before.

"Ooh baby," Tom says, lowering himself back onto the bed and grinning broadly.

"No! You don't *think*?" I say.

"Thwack – Aaah!" Tom giggles. "Sounds like Dante and the naughty policeman are having fun to me."

He snuggles towards me.

"Not sure it sounds like fun myself," I say.

"Who do you think is thwacking who?" Tom whispers.

We both listen again until the noise repeats. We snort and laugh together.

"It's got to be the policeman doing the thwacking, right?" I say.

Tom shrugs and pulls me towards him. "I don't know," he says, "But it makes me feel a bit..." As he says this, he reaches over and grabs my dick.

"Hey, don't start anything you can't handle, Mr Herpes," I warn him.

"I thought maybe you could..." His voice peters out, but he rolls onto his front and pulls me towards him, making it perfectly clear what he wants.

"But what about your..."

"It's fine," he says. "Just be gentle with me," he giggles.

I roll on top of him. "You sure?" I say.

"Mmmm," Tom coos. "I'm feeling really horny actually."

I reach for my wallet and pull out a condom and lube pack.

Then I rip the top off the sachet of lube with my teeth, and manoeuvre myself between Tom's legs. As I pull the condom on, I lean down to his ear. "Did I ever tell you?" I say, slipping a finger into his arse.

"Mmm?" he says.

"You have the best ideas in the *whole wide world.*"

"I kneel again and squirt the rest of the lube onto my dick. Behind me in the distance, I hear another whistle, followed by another grunt.

"Oooh baby," Tom says.

I grin broadly and move myself into position but then I pause – I've had a different idea. I lean forward so that my mouth is against Tom's ear.

"I didn't know you were into..." I whisper, as I sit up and straighten my arm for the swing.

Tom gasps in shock, and for a moment, I think I have slapped his arse too hard, but then he groans appreciatively, and writhes a little on the bed.

It's the breeze that wakes me. Tom has opened the windows on both sides of the van, and the tiny curtains are moving to and fro as it gusts back and forth. A tiny bird is chirruping merrily somewhere to my right; it is so loud it sounds as if it's inside the van.

I stretch and yawn happily. I feel amazingly relaxed this morning, in fact – I realise – it's the first time I have actually felt like I'm *on* holiday. I guess it always takes a while to settle into the rhythm.

I mention this to Tom, but he just giggles and says, "Just because you got a shag!"

I listen to the birdsong for a moment. "You know there's a French colloquial expression for grumpy, or bad tempered," I tell him. "They say *mal baisé.*"

He rolls over and props himself up on one elbow. "A bad fuck?" he asks.

"No, *badly* fucked," I correct him.

"So if someone's badly fucked it means he's in a bad mood?" Tom asks incredulously.

I laugh. "Well, they're a bit macho, so it's usually *she's* badly fucked," I say. *"Elle est mal baisée.* But yeah… it means she's in a bad mood, and by implication that she's in a bad mood because she needs a good shagging."

"Stunningly accurate," Tom says, rolling onto his back.

I shimmy slightly down the bed so that I can rest my head on his stomach.

"So did your poor dick survive the ordeal last night?" I ask.

Tom's chest jumps beneath me as he laughs. "Yes," he says. *"Tres bien baisé, merci."*

Hey I wonder if Dante is in a good mood too," I giggle.

Tom strokes my hair and judders again. "*I* wonder if he can *sit down*?" he says.

"What are we helping him with again?" I ask.

Tom shrugs. "Oh, yeah… Chickens or netting or something," he says.

When we arrive at the farmhouse, Dante's policeman friend is leaving, so we open the gate as he drives past and rather stupidly stand to attention. We both think it's funny, but he seems un-amused, and shouts something at Tom as he drives through.

"He says to make sure and shut the gate," Tom translates.

Dante is sitting at the kitchen table peering into a bowl of steaming coffee.

He looks up brightly and beckons us in. "Come, come!" he says, jumping up. "Coffee."

We take our seats and pour coffee from the pot. I remember that this is a no sugar zone, so I make sure Dante can't see the inside of my cup and serve the strict minimum – about half an inch.

"I'm glad you help today," Dante says, dunking a piece of bread into his coffee. "It's very hard for me..." He frowns. "When is only me," he adds doubtfully.

He looks rough this morning – his skin looks dry and wrinkled. His hair – though still jet black and shiny – is flattened on one side and jutting out on the other. His green eyes look a little redder around the edges than usual.

"It's hard to do it on your own," I say, in a slow, didactic voice.

Dante nods but seemingly misunderstands. "No," he says. "It's okay. I drink too much with Paolo."

"Paolo the Policeman," I say, thinking that it sounds like a Disney character.

Dante frowns. "You see Paolo?" he asks.

"Twice," Tom replies. "When we arrived, and today."

Dante's eyes narrow. He stares at his coffee and chews his bread. Tom glances at me and raises an eyebrow.

When Dante looks back up he looks me straight in the eye, as if challenging me to believe him. "My best friend," he says.

I nod and force a reassuring smile. "Friends are important," I say.

Dante bangs his chest. "Paolo has big heart," he says.

The job, it transpires, is to cover an unused chicken run with orange nylon netting.

Dante has decided – for reasons he explains at great length in Italian and which I don't understand or really care about – that the chickens need their own area. Presumably, the netting is required to make them stay put.

The run is about twenty meters long by three wide, bordered by a low brick wall supporting a fence.

We divide the labour, with Tom and I on each side of the run, wiring each loop of netting to a loop of the fence. Dante deals with cutting the lengths of netting and stretching them between Tom and myself as well as attaching the edges of the lengths together.

He's very specific about wanting a metal tie through *every* loop of the fence. If they're not *bionic* chickens then it seems a bit over the top to me, but, well, it's his fence and they are his chickens so I say nothing and with a dismayed glance at the length of the run, start to twist the first of the wire links.

It's a fiddly, repetitive task, and for the first fifteen minutes or so I feel resentful at having to spend my holiday doing such a shitty job to someone else's absurdly over-engineered specifications....

And yet...

And yet, I settle into the mindless rhythm of it, watching Tom on the far side, and Dante zigzagging between us.

I adjust my speed, going faster when I get behind, occasionally slowing down when I get ahead. The sun beats down making me sweat slightly, and every now and then, the breeze lifts up my t-shirt and blows refreshingly around my sweaty waist.

"You okay?" Dante asks, as he stretches the next length of netting to my outstretched hand.

I smile at him, a genuine smile born of team effort. "I *am* actually," I say, realising it as I say it. "It's nice."

Dante nods appreciatively, and pauses as if I should continue, so I frown and think about how I feel. "It's good to have something to do with your hands," I say. "Something manual... It kind of frees the mind."

Dante nods. "People meditate," he says. "They should come fix fences."

I nod. Meditative pretty much describes how I'm feeling. "Not a lot of manual work nowadays," I tell him. "Not in the city."

Dante pulls his tobacco pouch from his pocket and starts to roll a cigarette. "Yes," he says. "Work is key. Everyone want luxury – no work," he says.

I groan at the realisation that I have started him on one of his philosophical tangents again – a tangent I have already heard. It's not that I don't agree with him, but I was enjoying the non-mental space provided by the work. That's the whole point... The last thing I want is to intellectualise about *why* it's good.

"Sometimes I think I should make a, how you call that? *Una comunità hippy*," he says.

"A hippy commune?"

Dante nods. "Yes, you know just let city people come live here. Discover simple life."

I shrug noncommittally. "Why not?" I say.

Dante nods at me. "You think is good idea?" he asks.

I shrug again. "I guess," I say.

"Someone like you would want?" he asks.

"Me?" I frown and grin at the same time. "Not really my scene," I say, wrinkling my nose. "No communes for me... I like my own place, my own things..."

"But you enjoy today?" he says.

I nod and smile. "Sure, it's nice," I say.

Dante nods reflectively and hands me another bunch of metal ties, which I wedge between my teeth.

Thankfully, he then turns to Tom. "Toma!" he shouts. *"E' pronto per la prossima?"*

For nearly three hours we work like this. Dante and Tom chat in Italian, and I make no attempt to understand – in fact their voices drift and merge in with the background sounds of wind and trees and birdsong.

My mind wanders over the mundane and drifts to great questions of life and then bumps back down to the everyday again, strangely liberated by this simple task on this beautiful day.

Childhood places and people float to the surface – the seafront in Eastbourne, the taste of a '99 ice cream, an auntie's bent umbrella.

I think about the fact that we have no food and wonder where the nearest supermarket is, and I think about Dante living off the land, picking leeks when he wants leeks, killing a pig when he wants pork.

I think about Jenny and Sarah back in Nice, and the van, the van she bought with Nick, parked over the way in all its orange splendour. The van that Jenny conceived in because of my own accident, and I think of Steve, poor dead Steve. It's a shame he never met Tom... He would have liked him, except of course, if Steve were here then Tom wouldn't be.

I think about what *quality* means – and wonder if the simple repetitive satisfaction of what I'm doing is what people mean when they talk about quality of life... Most don't but maybe they should.

As I loop another piece of wire and twist it, I drift back into the physical and wonder what it is about that gesture – about the *clack* the cutter makes as it cuts off the raggedy ends – that is so very satisfying.

Dante is right in so many ways about so many things, and I wonder just why it is that I'm so resistant to having it all explained to me.

Is it what he's saying or the *way* he explains it. Or is it something underlying about Dante, something about his very *being* that I don't like.

I watch a tiny finch sitting on the fence a few meters back from where I am working and watch in amusement as it bobs up and down as I fiddle with the netting. I can't remember the last time I took the time to watch a bird sitting on a fence. I guess we really are in danger of losing this meditative quality from our modern lives. Maybe Dante's commune idea isn't so bad after all.

When I notice that the bird has gone, and I realise that I didn't see it fly away, I know that the last few minutes were in fact hours. I look at my hands, working away on their own, looping wire through the final link of the fence.

Tom and Dante are standing, hand on hips waiting for me.

I look at them there, standing side-by-side, smirking at me, presumably at some in-joke or maybe just at the fact that I've been so lost in my thoughts that I haven't noticed them.

Whatever the reason, some unnamed pang of emotion registers at the sight of them like that. On some, semi-conscious level, something is noticed; something is *noted*. I can't quite figure it out, but it's to do with them being together and me being the separate one. My stomach knots.

I finish twisting the two ends of the wire together and jump down.

After lunch I leave Tom and Dante herding chickens towards the pen, and head off to the local supermarket for provisions. The name of the store – Mec-Market – momentarily puts a smile back on my face. *Mec* is the French word for bloke. Mec-Market would be a great name for a gay bar, I decide.

I cross the scrubby car park and check out the front of the store. It bristles with brightly coloured rubber rings and inflatable crocodiles.

A woman in a pinny squints at me from a sun-lounger. As I reach the threshold I pause and she grins at me revealing a gold tooth.

"*Avanti,*" she says, waving me in.

Mec-Market is cavernous space. The light filtering past the inflatable toys is supplemented by four skylights, producing godly circles of light. Random goods within the store – a pile of filter-coffee machines here, a rack of faded seed packets there, a pile of green bananas over the far side, are lit by the beams. Dust particles dance and float in the columns of light.

The air is rich with smells: floor polish, soap, spices, rubber... There seems to be little logic to how the store is organised, so I zigzag up and down the isles, checking my list as I push past tins of tomatoes and sachets of weed killer, past bottles of shampoo and dog-leads.

Hung on hooks next to the nails and screws there's even what looks like a range of cock-rings, laid out from small to large. Every time I swing past the front window, the owner in her bed-chair looks up, winks and waves me on.

When I reach the checkout I peer outside. The sun has moved over and the owner has fallen asleep.

I load my shopping noisily onto the counter. I stand in the entrance and cough loudly. I even bump the trolley into the edge of her chair as I push it past, but nothing awakens her, so with a shrug I slump onto a deckchair.

"*When in Rome,*" I think.

Every few minutes a camper van rolls past followed by its personal mini-tailback. A mangy dog is sniffing around the edges of the car park. A skitty cat darts along the wall.

I wonder if Tom will kick up a fuss about leaving tomorrow. I know he's enjoying the stay at Dante's place, but how on earth can I explain to him that he's enjoying it just a bit *too* much?

There! The decision to leave appears to have been taken.

So I sit and ponder how to tell Tom that not all choices are good; that some choices preclude others. That getting closer to Dante may be the end of getting closer to me. How to explain that I can sense real danger without sounding hysterical and jealous?

I watch a green and orange rubber ring suspended from the awning as it bounces and rotates in the wind.

What I need, is a destination, an alibi, a positive reason why we have to leave... Something that we have to see, something it would be a shame to miss. I decide to get one of the maps next to the checkout and work something out.

When the bed-chair beside me creaks I look up to see the woman heading inside.

It's as if she has never been asleep. She moves behind the till and starts to work her way through the pile, lazily typing the price of each item, before loading it into a carrier bag.

It's funny how a tiny change to the way things are done can leave you ill at ease. I shuffle from one foot to the other as I wait for each completed bag to be handed to me.

"Camping?" she asks, waving a tin of tuna at me.

I nod and smile.

"*Inglese?*" she asks, nodding at the Volkswagen.

I nod again. "I live in France," I say. "*J'habite en France,*" I repeat hoping that French will be easier for her to understand.

She shrugs and places the tuna inside the carrier bag and reaches for one of the three corn-on-the-cobs.

"*Camping municipale?*" she asks. "*Vernazza?*"

I shake my head. "Full," I say. "Erm, *completo.*"

She nods and grins. "*Allora, Rommagiore,*" she says, pointing the corn on the cob at me accusingly.

I shake my head. "*Completo,*" I say.

The woman squints at me, then grins, apparently enjoying this game of guess-the-campsite. "*La Spezia?*" she says.

I shake my head and smile back.

She frowns in amused puzzlement, then shrugs.

"Farm," I say. "Erm, *Podere?*" I add. "*Camping completo,*" and she nods as though this explains everything.

"Signor Romero?" she asks.

I realise that I don't know Dante's surname, so I shrug and make an embarrassed grimace. *"Mi scusa,"* I say. *"Signor Dante."*

The woman thinks for a moment and – rather disgustingly – scratches her chin with the hairy end of the corn-cob she's holding.

"Fattoria Migliore?" she asks. *"Dante Migliore?"*

I shrug again, and the woman shrugs back, but the magical moment is lost, the energy has shifted and the game is over. She moves into triple speed, clearly decided to waste no more time on this stupid tourist who can't even describe where he's staying.

I pay her the twenty-seven euros and head out into the sunshine.

The car park shimmers in the heat. I load the bags into the van and slide the door shut.

The woman is watching me from beneath the *Mec-Market* sign. She has her hands on her hips. I climb into the driver's seat and gun the engine.

As I swing the van towards the exit, the woman steps forward, so I brake and stop. Gravel spits beneath the tyres.

She looks deadly serious so, wondering if I have made some terrible *faux-pas*, I lean out of the window.

She nods towards the east, towards Dante's place, and then shaking her head she says, *"Sta attento. E' brutta gente, la famiglia Migliore."*

I frown at her. *"Mi Scusa?"*

She tutts and rolls her eyes, then says, very slowly, *"Gentaglia, i Migliori…"*

I blink and shrug. "Sorry, I…" I say, shaking my head.

"Sta attento," she says, now nodding at me, raising a hand and wiggling a finger at me. Whatever she's saying she's not joking. *"E brutta gente…"* she says again.

Finally, realising that I'm not understanding a word, she turns back into the shadowy interior of the shop, and lets her hand drop dismissively to her side.

When I reach the farm, the gate is open, so I drive right up to the front of the house, then walk back and close the gate. I sneak a glimpse at the name on the letterbox - *Migliore*. Now *what* did she say? *Buttagenti*?

I close the gate, and as I return to the van, Tom bounds around the corner, grinning broadly. "You get everything?" he asks.

I wiggle my brow and throw open the side door of the van revealing the pile of carrier bags.

"Wow," Tom says. "All that?"

I nod. "I need to sort through it though… The checkout lady mixed it all up."

Tom peers inside a bag, then glances back at the farmhouse.

"What does *Statento* mean*?*" I ask him.

Tom frowns. "*Sta attento*?" he says. "Erm, *be careful*… why?"

"And *Butagenta*?" I ask him. "Only she said something – the lady in the shop - and I couldn't work it out."

"Butagenta?" Tom repeats, shaking his head and pushing out his lips. "Sorry," he says. "What was she talking about? What was the context?"

I shrug. "If I knew that…" I say.

"Yeah, well… Sorry, can't help you then," Tom says, glancing nervously back at the farmhouse. "Erm, can I… Only, we're killing chickens."

I wrinkle my nose. "*Killing chickens*! Tom! That's disgusting."

Tom looks at me uncomprehendingly, as if to be killing chickens is the most natural thing in the world for a vegetarian to be doing.

"It's not actually," he says. "It's like the man says… it just depends how you do it."

"All the same, Tom," I protest. "You're supposed to be vegetarian."

Tom shrugs. "I may even eat chicken tonight," he says. "I mean, if you can kill one, then why not?"

I sigh and shake my head. "Whatever," I say. "Enjoy yourself."

Tom smiles at me. "Enjoy might be a bit strong," he says. "But it is interesting."

"Tom, before you go?" I say.

He pauses, one hand on the edge of the door and looks back at me. "Yeah?"

"Can we move on tomorrow," I say. "Please?"

Tom thinks about this and then shrugs dismissively. "Nah, not tomorrow," he says.

I would argue, but there's no one to argue with.

In an attempt at calming my mounting anger, I stomp around the perimeter fence. I argue with myself – point and counterpoint – trying to be reasonable, trying to see both sides of the story.

I tell myself that Tom's answer may have been a little dismissive, but it wasn't truly aggressive. I force myself to acknowledge that I *did* ask him the question, I did say, *can* we leave tomorrow? No *is* a valid response.

But it doesn't really work; it doesn't really quell the rage. Sure, it contains it momentarily; it stops it bursting out all over the shop. It stops me running over to the two of them and telling them to fuck off, or simply getting in the van and driving right home. But the rage remains, compressed into a manageable sized lump, right in the middle of my rib cage.

At the end of the field I use the compost hillock to climb back over the fence, noting vaguely that Tom or Dante, or Tom *and* Dante, have dug a new hole next to it. Presumably they are intending to add a new batch of compost, or pig carcasses, or whatever it is that Dante dumps here.

The forest is as eerily calm as the first time, only now the strange silence entices me further in. I head down the corridor of trees listening to the spongy crunching noise of pine needles beneath my feet, listening to see if I am yet far enough away to escape the voices of Tom and Dante on the farm behind me.

Eventually I come to a recently felled clearing, and sit on a pile of stripped logs and wish for the first time in years that I still smoked.

It's just after six when Tom returns to the van. "What have you been up to then?" he asks cheerfully.

The words, *quietly smouldering*, come to mind, but instead, when I open my mouth, what comes out is, "Oh, not much, wandering around the forest." I even manage a fraudulent smile.

"And you?" I ask. "Looks like you've been digging ditches?"

Tom frowns at me cutely, and says, "No, planting zucchini and aubergines actually."

"Zucchini," I say. "How American of you."

Tom shrugs and grins. "Or courgettes..." he says. "You know what I mean... Anyway they're called *zucchini* in Italian." He stretches and pulls a face. "My back's killing me though... I might get you to massage it later."

"*Might* you now," I say, forcing a smile to make my reply look like a joke.

"Later though," he says, reaching for a towel. "I need to go and shower, and Dante is making dinner for us."

I nod silently and stare at him.

"Is that okay?" he asks. "I *said* it was okay," he adds tentatively.

I can't even begin to think of a way to explain to his innocent little face just how *not* okay it is. I can't believe we can be so out of sync. So I say, "Sure, that'll be dandy."

Tom plants a peck on my unresponsive lips. He smells of soil.

"*Is* that okay?" he tries again, confused by part of my response, by some leaking air of grievance he has detected.

"Go shower," I say. "I'll meet you there."

Unable to face Dante on my own, I tidy the van, occasionally glancing out of the side window until I see Tom, heading for the farmhouse – the wet towel draped around his shoulders.

I take a deep breath, swallow hard and head across the field, telling myself as I walk that it's just not fair to blame Tom for not reading my mind, that it's not his fault he can't sense the turmoil within. But even if I don't blame him, the fact that he has no idea – and I mean absolutely *no* idea what I'm thinking... Well, that must mean *something* about our relationship, right?

I push into the kitchen a few seconds after Tom, but already he and Dante are chatting in Italian. I stand at the entrance until they notice my presence. Dante crosses the room and kisses me on the cheek without interrupting his flow of words. The gesture shocks me a little, and I frown and resist the desire to wipe my cheek.

"So what's today's subject?" I ask moving to Tom's side.

"Oh, we've been talking about religion all day," Tom tells me. "Well, religion and how to grow zucc... Sorry, *courgettes*."

"Religion?"

"Yeah, we got onto the whole Judaeo-Christian monogamy thing," Tom says.

"Right," I say, walking towards the stove and peering in at the swirling spaghetti.

"Dante doesn't believe in monogamy," Tom says.

Dante stirs the pot and glances up at me, flashing his teeth. It could be a smile or it could be a primitive baring of teeth, it's hard to say.

"Tom says you are quite old fashion," Dante tells me.

"Old fashion," I repeat. I bite my lip and nod. "*Does* he now?"

Tom steps sideways so that his hip is touching mine. It's a tiny sign of solidarity but it does what he intends; it placates me. "I didn't *exactly* say that," he says. "I said you believe in monogamy, it's *Dante* thinks that's old fashioned."

"Old fashion and stupid," Dante says.

I raise an eyebrow, and sigh, realising that it's going to be even harder than I thought keeping my ball of rage contained.

"*Stupid…*" I repeat flatly.

Dante pours the spaghetti into a strainer and through a cloud of steam, he adds, "Well, for a homosexual."

The phrase is such a shock that I have to pause to catch my breath. The subject matter, the frankness of the delivery – well, it all implies an intimacy that Dante and I simply don't have.

"If you say so," I say, turning the phrase over in my mind. The word *homosexual* grates too – in my experience, people who say *homosexual* are rarely very comfortable with *homosexuality*.

I bite my bottom lip. A response is forming, but I hesitate. Then I think, "*What the hell.*"

"So what kind of a homosexual are *you* then Dante?" I ask.

He stops stirring and shoots me a glare. I can see that he has stopped breathing. Then he looks back at the pan before him and slowly exhales. "So tonight," he says, suddenly all upbeat. "*Spaghetti con Pomodori.*"

I restrain a smirk at the change of subject. "Tomato," I say, tilting my head slightly. "Yum." My voice is perfect. I could be taking the piss but then again I could be being perfectly genuine.

Tom smiles at me vaguely as if all of this is passing him by.

"*And when did Tom's radar get so cloudy?*" I wonder.

It's not until the end of the thankfully short meal that everything becomes clear, or at least a little clearer.

Tom is washing dishes to my left; I am drying a plate with Dante's slightly surreal *Charles and Diana* tea towel.

Tom jokingly barges me with his hip as he scrubs a pan, and I glance over my shoulder to see if Dante – who is seated at the table rolling a cigarette – is watching us. I see him reach into a tin box and sprinkle something on top of the tobacco he has laid out.

He must sense my gaze because he looks up and smiles lopsidedly. "I grow it here," he says. "Tom show you my plant?"

My hands pause their plate-wiping action. "No," I say. "He didn't. *Funny that*." I tip my head to one side and raise an eyebrow at Tom who shrugs naively.

"Hey, we only smoked, like, one joint," he says.

"Two," Dante says behind me. "Today two." He looks at me. "Tom says you no like."

I shake my head. "Dope makes me paranoid," I say. *"So Tom and Dante are sharing drugs now,"* I think.

"*More* paranoid," Tom mumbles.

"Okay, *more* paranoid," I agree.

Once the boys have shared another joint I end up feeling paranoid anyway. The conversation takes on a dreamlike edge – the out-of-phase thing between Tom and I exacerbated so much by the drug that I start to wonder if dope isn't the simple explanation for *all* the misunderstandings of the last few days.

The conversation wanders and Tom, touchingly, does his best to translate and keep me involved. But though they can't hear it themselves, the level of the conversation is so base, the theories so formulaic, the logic so *stoned*, that I simply can't be bothered to get involved.

Tom and Dante are all loved-up on shared hard-labour and grass, so I let them carry on and satisfy myself thinking about other places and other times and watching their faces in the flickering light.

I think about Jenny and Sarah back in Nice. I remind myself that this strange looks-so-good dream of Tom and Dante and myself, sitting in a farmhouse in the flickering light of an oil lamp on a beautiful summer's evening... this stranger than strange dream which is, in reality, a nightmare of manipulation and power games and dodgy philosophy... Well, it's all bearable because it will soon be over.

"So?" Dante says. He's nodding my way. "What does old fashion boy think?"

I look from Dante's face to Tom's and skew my eyebrows.

"It's old fashion*ed*," I correct him, unable to bear it any longer. "I'm afraid I wasn't really listening," I say shaking my head. "I was... elsewhere."

"Dante is saying that, you know, a committee should decide who can have children and who can't," Tom says. "That some parents..."

"*Most*," Dante interrupts.

Tom nods. "Sorry, *most* parents shouldn't be allowed to have kids because they don't, you know, have the skills to bring them up properly."

I nod in a non-committal way.

Tom shrugs and smiles. "I can think of a few people who shouldn't!" he laughs.

I shrug.

"I thought you'd, you know, have a point of view," Tom says. Then with a wry smile he adds, "A *different* point of view."

I shrug again. "It sounds pretty fascistic," I say, saying my thoughts as they form. "It sounds like you're setting yourself up to be arbiter of someone else's human rights – the right to have children."

Tom frowns.

"*Ze people's committee vill decide*," I say.

Dante smiles and shrugs. His eyes have become heavy lidded slits.

"*Fascista*," he says. "You know it means very different thing to Italian. *Fascista* not always mean bad in Italy."

"I think you could find a few people in England who would agree," I say. "They wouldn't be *my* friends though."

Tom swivels his frown back at me. It's as if the edgy aggression of the conversation is finally piercing his dope-bubble.

"I think Italian peoples, maybe Latin peoples... More comfortable with the idea that all is not good, all is not bad," Dante says.

I really can't be bothered trying to debate this in Pidgin English with two slightly drunk, *very* stoned sparring partners, so I just shrug again.

"Anglo-Saxons are much more…" He makes a chopping action with his hand. "This good, that bad," he says.

"Black and white," Tom says.

"Italians, Latins… we say everything is good and bad at same time," Dante continues.

"Except certain parents," I say, unable to resist. "Who are *so* bad they shouldn't be allowed to have children."

Dante shrugs and nods. "Maybe."

"And what about, I don't know, say, the *Holocaust*?" I add. "Hitler's extermination of, like, however many millions of Jews and Gypsies and *homosexuals*… That was good *and* bad too, yes?"

Dante pushes his lips out and frowns and shrugs and smiles all at once. It means, *well, of course, you can always find exceptions…*

"Or Aids," I say. "Presumably you can see the good in that as well can you?"

Tom frowns heavily now and reaches out to touch my hand. "All Dante's saying…" he says.

"I understand *perfectly* what he's saying," I interrupt. "*I'm* not stoned."

"Aids!" Dante snorts.

"It's just that none of it stands up to analysis," I mumble. " You can't go around saying everything is this or that if it isn't. It's pointless."

"Aids is not even real disease," Dante says. He nods his chin at me. "You believe in Aids?" he asks. He turns to Tom. "You?"

I open my mouth to speak, then close it again and stand.

"That's it," I say as neutrally as I can. "I'm turning in," I add, faking a yawn.

Dante smiles at me superciliously, as if he has won. He looks like he thinks I'm running away.

I wonder for a moment if he isn't right, but on reflection I'm clear about my motivation. I don't *need* to argue with Dante because I don't need to convince him. I don't *care* what Dante thinks.

Tom stands and rubs Dante's shoulder affectionately, then straightens and latches onto my arm. "Me too," he says. "I'm knackered."

"*We* work very hard," Dante says, pointedly gesturing that he means Tom and himself.

I steer Tom towards the door. "Come on my little dope-head," I say. "Let's get you home."

As we cross the field Tom stumbles against my side, snorts, then starts to giggle. I put an arm around his shoulders and guide him through the gate.

"What?" I ask.

Tom snorts again and I start to smile – the first genuine smile of the evening.

"Come on," I say. "Out with it…"

Tom shrugs. "Oh, just you and Dante," he says. "Sniping at each other."

I glance over at the van and correct our trajectory by steering Tom a little to the left. "And that's *funny*?" I say.

Tom looks sideways at me and gives me his lopsided cheeky smile. Then he nods in front at the trees and says, "Wow, have you seen how big the trees are tonight?"

I look at the trees and it's strange to say, but he's right. In the peculiar monotone moonlight they do look bigger than by day.

"Yeah," I say, and giggle at the absurdity of the proposition, "they *are* big tonight."

Back in the van Tom sits like a man who's had a lobotomy, his hands dangling loosely between his legs. He watches me slot the bed together.

He's completely stoned and more than a little drunk, but the wry smile and the blank regard give him the innocent air of a six year old. His inexplicable surge of cuteness causes a tiny fist of loving angst to form just below my throat, making it hard to swallow, and pushing my earlier anger aside.

He stands and, giggling, he lets me undress him. I push him forward onto the bed, where he flops corpse-like.

"Massage," he mumbles.

I yawn and shuck my jeans. "I'm not sure about that," I say. "I'm knackered too." But that's not the real reason of course… I'm just not sure that I've forgiven him for…

I momentarily can't remember what I'm angry about – I'm a little drunk myself. The reason is lurking on the edges of my consciousness – firmly within reach – but I decide to leave it be, for tonight at least.

"Massage!" Tom repeats childishly.

I pull my t-shirt over my head and straddle his legs.

"Well, seeing as it's you," I say.

He makes a *humm* sound, and wriggles and settles on the bed beneath me.

I reach for a tube of suntan lotion and squirt a little onto his back, then slowly start to run the edges of my thumbs along his vertebrae.

"Oh yeah," he murmurs.

I smile and press a little harder, moving my thumbs up towards his shoulders, and as I do so my semi-erect dick touches Tom's buttocks. He wiggles slightly and spreads his legs a little.

"A *massage* you said," I chide.

With visible effort Tom lifts his head and peers back at me. "Yeah, a *full* massage," he smirks.

A dog barks in the distance reminding me that the sliding panel of the van is still open behind me. "I just need to close that door," I say setting a foot onto the floor of the van. "Keep the mosquitoes out."

I freeze, one knee still on the bed. My eyes widen and my throat constricts. I make a little gasping sound.

I grab a pillow to hide my erect dick. Dante is standing silently just outside the van. He has his feet firmly planted, and his arms crossed.

"What the fuck," Tom says, rolling sideways and pulling a sheet across himself.

Dante uncrosses his arms and thrusts something at me. "Tom forget," he says.

I reach out and pull Tom's wallet from his grasp. "You made me jump," I say.

Dante nods and grins salaciously. "I know," he says. "I see."

I hand the wallet behind me to Tom who frowns and blinks slowly.

"Thanks Dante," I say. "*Goodnight.*"

But Dante doesn't move.

Tom sits up straighter. It's a clear effort to straighten his mind. "Is there a problem?" he asks.

Dante grins dumbly and shakes his head, and I remember that he too is completely stoned.

"*Goodbye* Dante," I say forcefully. I reach for the handle to the door.

"Buonanotte," Tom says.

Dante nods and starts to turn and I slide the heavy door across. He glances back at us one last time before shuffling off across the field.

"Jesus!" I exclaim.

Tom nods at me, wide-eyed.

"How long was *he* there?" I say. "And how did he get your wallet?"

"Weird," Tom says.

I sigh unhappily. *"Yeah,"* I say, pulling a face. "Weirder by the minute, did you *see* the way he just stood there?"

Tom shrugs and throws himself back on the bed. "He's just stoned," he says. "He probably feels lonely. He probably wanted to join in," he says repositioning himself for the resumption of his massage.

"Hey! Tom!" I say, prodding him so that he looks at me. "He probably *did* want to, and that's not okay. *Right?*"

"Right," Tom says, his voice gently mocking. "Massage?" he adds hopefully. "Please?"

Tom's hangover is worse than mine, so I get up and make the coffee.

"Just put it on the side," he tells me. "I'll be up in a bit."

It's hazy today and the diffused sunlight makes everything uniformly blinding.

I grab my sunglasses from the dashboard and sit on the step of the van. After a few minutes, realizing that Tom has fallen back to sleep, I move outside and settle in the shade. One of Dante's cocks is screaming a belated dawn chorus and I can hear a vague sound of hammering.

When Tom finally appears the first thing I spot is that he's wearing yesterday's dirty work clothes.

"You're not helping Dante again are you?" I ask. "I mean, you're completely knackered..."

Tom sits on the step and starts to tie his shoelaces. "He needs help," he says with a shrug.

I put down *Gay Times* and stand and move to his side. "Hey Mister," I say. "Don't forget you're on holiday."

Tom nods glumly. "Yeah, I know," he says. "But, it's good for me really. It's different - it's like they say, a change is as good as a rest."

I nod and rub his back. "Sure, but why not actually *have* a rest?" I say. "Dante managed fine before we turned up."

Tom sighs. "Well, just about," he says. "You've seen the state of the place."

"And he'll have to manage tomorrow once we've left," I say. *"Funny,"* I think. *"I was wondering how to say that..."*

I brace myself for a fight but Tom surprises me by saying, "Yeah, I suppose." He runs a hand through his hair and yawns and stretches. "Look, I'll go over and get this done," he says. "And then maybe we can..." A shadow sweeps across his face. "Tomorrow?" he says. "Since when?"

I shrug. "Since I had enough of here, I suppose."

Tom leans back against the van, his features dark and brooding. "And what about me?" he says.

"Tom, we *have* to move on at some point, and there's loads of other stuff I want to do."

"Like what?"

I shake my head slowly in exasperation. "Like visit La Spezia, like going to see the lake at Como... I'm sorry, but I don't want to spend my whole holiday on a bloody farm."

"But why not?" Tom says. "I like it here."

"Tom, I know you do," I say earnestly, "and I *accept* that, and that's why we've been here for three days now. But you also have to accept that *I* want to move on. I want to do other stuff, and I want some time alone with you."

"But how often do you meet someone like Dante?" Tom protests. "How often do you meet someone you really connect with like that?"

I bite my lip and take a deep breath. "Tom, why are you being like this? I *don't* connect with Dante. You know that. I just *don't*. And his snooping around peering in at us only makes me like him less."

Tom looks like a four year old. He looks like he might stamp his feet in anger. "I understand that you don't like Dante," he says. "I do. But I'm not ready to leave. I want to make the most of this. I want to get to know him better before we leave. I want to experience more of this whole living off the land thing, I want..."

"Tom," I interrupt. "You can't just..."

Tom shakes his head. "Look, it's not complicated," he says. "I'm not leaving tomorrow."

"You're not?" I say. "So you have a veto now, do you?"

He glances away towards the forest and then down at his feet. He kicks the side of one foot with the other. "I think you're being unreasonable," he says without looking up.

"*Unreasonable?*" I repeat.

"Yeah, just because, you... I mean, don't you think we should discuss what we're doing? Instead of you just *deciding*?"

"The way you consulted with me when you told Dante we would help him yesterday?" I point out. "*And* again today? Is that the sort of discussion..."

"Consult?" Tom spits. "*Consult* with you? What are you, like my bank manager or something?"

I frown at him. There's no real logic to the argument, and I'm left speechless. I wave my hands vaguely and shrug.

"Consult!" Tom repeats, as if it's the most absurd word he ever heard.

"So when do *you* want to leave?" I say as evenly as I can. "I mean, we can't stay here forever, even you agree that, *right*?"

Tom frowns and swallows hard. "I don't know," he says. "I like it here."

"What exactly do you like?" I say. "The farm or cute little Dante? Or is it the all-you-can-smoke dope? You didn't even tell me about that, by the way."

Tom shakes his head. "It's not that. It's... I don't know. I feel... I feel centred here. That's it. I feel more *me* here. And I really like working with Dante. I haven't felt this happy since..."

"It's *just* a holiday," I say. "It's just the first stop in a whole..."

"I wouldn't mind staying here the whole time," Tom says quietly.

"The *whole time*?" I repeat incredulously. "For a whole *month*?"

We stand and stare at each other in silence for a moment.

"It's not what you think," Tom says.

I laugh bitterly. "What do I *think* then? Please tell me."

"*Allora, Toma!*" As he rounds the corner Dante's voice jars the air with its boisterous optimism. When he reaches the van he grins lopsidedly and then, looking between our faces, his expression slips into a frown. "*Qualche Problema?*" he asks.

Tom stares at his feet and kicks at a stone. "*Mark vuole partire domani,*" he says.

"*Domani?!*" Dante repeats turning to look at me. "You leave tomorrow?"

I shrug. "It's a holiday," I say. "There are places to visit, things to see."

"But not tomorrow," Dante says. It sounds more like a statement than a protest.

I nod earnestly. "Sorry," I say. "I want to go to La Spezia, and to..."

"*La Spezia!*" Dante laughs dismissively. He spins on his heels and heads back towards the farmhouse.

"*Si puo' andare a La Spezia e tornare in giornata,*" he says, adding as he disappears from view. "*Un ora in ciascun senso.*"

Tom glares at me. I shrug.

Tom shakes his head. "Dante says La Spezia is just a day trip from here."

I try and calm my anger by pursing my lips and blowing.

"He says it's an hour each way," Tom continues.

"This isn't about a day trip, Tom," I say. "I want out of here. Can't you just trust me on this? Just once?" I say.

Tom grimaces. "Why should I?" he says. "You don't seem to trust me."

"Sometimes there are just things that you know. And I know we need to leave."

"I'm staying," Tom says.

"So what do we do – split up?" I say. "Do you really want that?"

Tom shakes his head. We stand in silence for a moment, absorbing the enormity of the moment.

"Look," Tom eventually says. "Let me help Dante out again tomorrow, and then we'll *both* go on Tuesday, okay?"

I sigh heavily.

"Where's the problem with that?" he asks. "I mean, it's not like we're short on time, is it?"

I shake my head sadly. "It's just…" I say. But my voice fades away. I've run out of steam.

Tom opens his mouth to say something, but then he closes it again. He glances over towards the farm, then turns back to face me. "Look, I have to go," he says. "Do what you want."

"What *I want*?"

"Yeah," he says. "Either go to La Spezia on your own tomorrow, or we'll go together on Tuesday."

Then he shrugs and walks away.

I slouch around all day, moving between the inside of the van and the deckchair outside. I'm too irritated to relax, too tired and annoyed to actually do anything.

Twice I catch a glimpse of Tom in the distance carrying something into the farmhouse but he doesn't even glance over at me.

Just before seven the dilemma of dinner starts to loom. I should obviously cook something for both of us, but I have this overriding feeling that Tom isn't coming back for dinner. I know from experience how he hates conflict – he'd do anything rather than come back for round two.

I'm peering into the cupboards, looking blankly at a pack of pasta and drumming my fingers on the worktop when Dante leans in through the door.

"Marco," he says brightly.

I turn slowly. "Dante," I say.

"You come eat with us, yes?"

I blink at him slowly. The idea that Dante and Tom are suddenly *us*, the idea that *I* am being invited to eat with *them* makes my blood boil. The edges of my vision actually cloud a little.

"Where's Tom?" I say.

Dante shrugs. "He is watching cook," he says. "We make big omelette. He wants you come now."

I nod. "*Does* he?" I say sarcastically.

Dante nods. "Yes," he says.

In a stalling tactic, I turn back and finger the pasta pack for a second. "Maybe you could ask him to come over here," I say flatly. "I think we need to talk." I glance back at Dante.

"You must stop," Dante says. "You make Tom angry."

I close my eyes and take a deep breath, then turn to face him full on. "Stop what?" I say.

Dante smiles and shrugs. "Tom knows what he want, you know what you want. Sometimes is different."

I shake my head slowly. "Dante," I say. "I really don't think we need any relationship advice from you. We were doing just fine, and…"

Dante shakes his head and interrupts me. "Not, not fine…" he says. "You force Tom to do things, he tell me. But…"

"Dante, butt out," I say.

Dante's smile finally fades. "But?" he repeats.

"Not your business," I say.

"Tom is my friend," Dante tells me. "And if Tom wants to stay some days more here on the farm…"

The clouding around my vision returns. In fact, I realise, it's taking on a red tinge – never a good sign.

"You want to see tourist place, buy t-shirts, you can go on your own but…"

I shake my head and interrupt. "Dante," I say. "I'm not being clear enough here, am I?"

Dante nods at me earnestly to continue.

"What I mean is…"

Dante raises an eyebrow. "Yes Marco?"

"What I mean is…" I say. I can hear my heartbeat pounding in my ear. "Fuck off!" I say.

Dante smiles strangely. I think he's trying to create a benign turn-the-other-cheek smile, but it looks more like a sneer. "Okay Marco," he says in a voice slimy with deceit. "I tell Tom you don't come for dinner then," he says.

I nod and step forward. "Yes," I say. "You tell him that."

Dante nods and lowers his foot from the step.

"Oh, and Dante," I say as he walks away.

He glances back but continues walking slowly.

"It's Mark," I say. "My fucking name is Mark!"

Dante smiles and shrugs and walks away.

I cook pasta for one and eat half. I sit and alternate between imagining punching that smile off Dante's face and worrying what he's saying to Tom.

When Tom finally returns to the van just after midnight, not a word is spoken. He undresses but keeps his underpants on. It's Tom's version of the Berlin wall, clearly stating, "*Stay away*".

Amazingly he manages to climb into the narrow double bed without brushing against me.

The next morning, I'm unable even to look him in the eye. Breakfast feels like a rubber band about to snap – and though I try out various conversational scenarios in my mind, they all ultimately come down to, *"Are you really going to choose Dante over me?"*

When Tom reappears from the van wearing yesterday's dirty work clothes, I no longer need to ask the question.

"You're helping Dante again," I say, as neutrally as possible.

Tom nods. "I said I was," he says. "So I am."

I nod silently.

"And you, you're going to La Spezia?" he asks flatly.

I shrug. "I'm tired," I say. "I didn't sleep well."

Tom nods and winks at me. "You worry too much," he says.

The wink softens my mood, and I wonder in a moment of self-doubt if I'm not making mountains out of molehills.

"I think I'll just kick back today," I say. "You know Tom, about last night…" I say.

But Tom gives me a tight smile, the slightest of waves and walks away. As he goes he says, "Don't worry about it. It's all Okay."

I sit and stare a little numbly at the space where he stood. The fact that Tom is apparently forgiving me makes me furious anew. I've no real desire to go to La Spezia on my own, but the idea of sitting here while they work the farm, or giving in and going and helping them, well, none of the options seem even remotely desirable.

My stomach is knotted, and not really knowing where I'm going or why, I pack up the chairs, lay them in the rear of the van, and climb into the driver's seat.

I realise that there's something slightly provocative about taking the chairs with me. Tom could doubt, could worry that I'm not coming back... I suppose I hope he *does*.

"Actually," I think furiously. *"I hope he shits himself at the idea that I have fucked off with his passport, his clothes, his money..."* When I reach the end of the lane, I even pause. The idea suddenly seems appealing… simply turn right and go home?

But then my mood softens again. If Tom is going to have a last chance, then fairness dictates that he be warned, that he take that decision knowingly.

I take a deep breath and wrench the wheel to the left.

Mindlessly I follow the signs towards La Spezia. Just after Romaggiore, the last of the five coastal towns, I come to a decision-time roundabout with three possible exits, one towards the Autostrada and home, another for La Spezia, and a third marked Campiglia. The sign for Campiglia carries a drawing of the mediaeval town centre.

My tiredness makes me hesitate. I'm not really sure I can face a day in the city, so I drive once again around the roundabout.

I could go back now and give Tom his last chance right away. But he's with Dante right now, and it really has to be discussed one-on-one.

I drive round again and consider the La Spezia exit. Finally when another VW van joins the roundabout and spins off towards Campiglia, I follow.

The town of Campiglia nestles against a tree-covered hill and with the ever-present backdrop of the Mediterranean it looks stunning. A tall crane overlooking the harbour gives the town a genuine workaday feel. I wish, with a pang of regret, that Tom were here to explore the shady streets with me.

I park the van in the sandy car park, and wander through to the sea front. The sea is sparkling and a sea breeze is whipping up frothy whitecaps.

Families are setting up along the beach, putting up windbreaks and throwing pebbles into the sea. Another reminder of what a holiday is supposed to be like.

As I walk past a phone box, a North African wearing a fluorescent orange djellabah, steps out. He smiles at me and unravels a roll of fake watches. It's the same stuff they sell in Ventimiglia; the same stuff they seem to sell everywhere in fact.

I shake my head and, apparently convinced, the man shrugs and walks away. The door to the phone-box catches the wind and hangs open and, without really deciding to, I step inside.

Jenny answers immediately, and tells me that she is just about to step out of the door. But picking up the urgency in my voice, she phones me back and listens patiently. It's hard to explain to a third party what's going on, and by trying to do so, I realise that, other than the simple fact of our derailed holiday plans, most of what's happening comes down to nothing more than an unnameable suspicion, an inexplicable lack of trust, a curious all-pervading feeling that Dante isn't what Dante appears to be.

By the end of the conversation, I'm so surprised at just how little I have to go on or explain, that I'm fully expecting Jenny to tell me to stop being stupid. But she doesn't say that at all.

"You listen to your feelings," she tells me. "You go with your intuition. And if you need to get Tom out of there, then go back and bloody get him. *Make* him leave."

I wonder if I haven't oversold my case. "But what if I'm wrong," I argue. "What if Dante truly is just a lovely generous hippy philosopher."

"Hey, if you *are* wrong," Jenny says. "Then Tom will lose a few extra days at the farm and gain some time somewhere else instead. It's hardly a drama. It sounds like he's being a completely selfish twat to me anyway, so he probably deserves it."

After the phone call I head to the nearest bar and order a double espresso. I take the most sheltered table against the transparent windbreak, but the wind is still strong enough to blow the tassels of the Orangina parasol wildly from side to side.

The waitress is miserable and unfriendly – the first truly unpleasant service I have ever had in Italy. Ignoring my attempts to speak Italian and superciliously speaking perfect English with an American twang, she takes my order.

I stare at the sea and think about Tom. I wonder if he really is falling in love with Dante. If he is then maybe there's no real hope for us anyway.

I finger a flyer on the table, and then slide it out from under the ashtray and idly turn it towards me. Silvio Berlusconi beams out at me. The photo shows him standing with a group of children beneath the Italian flag. *Forza Italia,* is emblazoned across the top of the flyer.

When the waitress returns she clatteringly dumps my coffee on the table before me. "That's three euro," she says, clearly wanting to be paid immediately.

While I fumble for change, she slides the flyer towards her across the table. "Yours?" she asks.

I pull a five-euro note from my wallet and glance up at her. I shake my head. "No," I say. "It was here on the table."

She screws the flyer into a ball and lobs it over the windbreak. As she swipes the five-euro note from my hand and walks away, she mutters disdainfully, *"Berlusconi! Ma! Forza Italia! Pff! Brutta gente!"*

Suddenly I'm finding her more interesting. When she returns with my change I smile broadly at her. "You speak very good English," I say.

She puts a hand on one hip and looks at me dourly. "I'm doing a degree," she says. "English and French. This is just for money."

I force my widest smile. "Well, it's very good," I tell her. "I speak French too... I live in Nice," I say.

She pushes her bottom lip out and nods, still all attitude. She starts to turn away.

"Hey, before you go, can you just tell me something?" I ask.

She pauses and turns back to look at me, too lazy or disinterested to fully interrupt the movement of her body towards the door.

"You said *brutagente*," I said.

She frowns at me and shrugs.

"What does *brutagente* mean?"

She shrugs again and grimaces. "*Brutta gente,*" she says, clearly correcting my dreadful pronunciation. "He's a prick," she says. "Berlusconi is a crook."

I nod, and then speaking quickly before she moves away, I add, "So *brutta gente* means what exactly? A crook?"

She frowns at me and shrugs. "*Ugly people... bad people.*"

"So if a family was *brutte gente?*" I say. "That would be what? Like, a bad family?"

She nods. "Yeah, I guess."

I nod. "But bad in what way?"

She wrinkles her nose and frowns at me as if I am completely deranged. "How would *I* know?" she says.

As I drive back, my sense of urgency – my feelings of illogical non-specific stress – grow exponentially.

Sure, the Mec-Market woman's comments could be nothing more than a local feud between families. Italian families are famous for their long-running feuds aren't they? It could all mean nothing at all.

But somehow, added to my all-pervading anxiety, my natural distrust of Dante's motives, well, it seems that in some way everything is slotting into place. It's like one of those game-shows where an object is slowly revealed... the picture is starting to come into view, and I though I don't yet know what it's of, I'm sure it's not nice.

The question remains, how to get this across to Tom without sounding hysterical and paranoid.

I park the van in its usual spot and climb down. I wait a moment, half-expecting Tom to come and greet me. I need a chance to talk to him alone, but no one comes. All is quiet.

I walk to the farmhouse - still no sign of life. I cross the front of the building and head towards the chicken house. Only clucking chickens greet me.

The door of the pig-shed is locked shut with a padlock, which strikes me as peculiar. The pigs are silent too, and in fact, I realise,

I have never heard a pig the whole time we have been on this farm. Could Dante have killed them *all*?

Somewhat pointlessly, I rattle the padlock and then continue on around the building, past the outside bathroom and on round to the front of the house. I shrug and try the door but it too is locked.

I rack my brain trying to remember what Tom said they were doing today, but I can't for the life of me remember.

"And what could they be doing anywhere but here?" I wonder. Dante doesn't even have a car.

I loop around the buildings, again, this time shouting Tom's name at every corner, my sense of disquiet growing.

I cup my ears and scan the horizon, but I hear only a crow squawking, the chickens clucking, a wasp buzzing by. As I walk back to the van, I glance at my watch. It's just after three. They won't be expecting me till at least 5 PM; I'll just have to wait.

But something's not right; my reliable old intuition sensors tell me so. I have to admit that I've sometimes been wrong. But I've often been spot on too. I start to chew my nails.

I slide open the van door and grab the kettle to make tea, but the water-pump spits and gurgles and spins into a high-speed whine, so I move all of the bedding out of the way and pull the translucent tank from under the sink. It's empty, so I head off back towards the farmhouse.

It won't fit between the tap and the washbasin, so I unscrew the showerhead and use the tube as a filling hose. The pipes clang and judder as the tank starts to fill and I sit on the step and stare out across the fields and wonder again where on earth Tom and Dante could have got to. The banging pipes remind me of the plumbing in our childhood home, and I try vaguely to work out why plumbing does that, then give up and put it down to a vague concept of "airlocks."

I check the tank, and when I see that it's only slightly filled, I realise how much it holds and just how heavy it's going to be to carry. So with another sigh, as if this is the hardest thing in the world, I set off to fetch the van, calculating as I walk that five gallons must weigh about twenty kilos.

It's a beautiful day. The air seems cleaner today and the light is harsh and white, the shadows deep and sharp. I wish the holiday were turning out differently. I wish Tom and I were in a boring campsite somewhere, heading out for a nice walk together and a simple picnic in a forest.

And something *is* wrong, I'm sure of it now. The physical sensations of 'something wrong' – the tightness in the chest, the sick stomach, the pulsing of my heart... I can feel it all happening as I walk.

"Maybe someone had an accident," I think. *"Maybe Dante had to take Tom to hospital."* He was playing with a chainsaw only yesterday after all.

When I get back with the van, the container is two-thirds full and the pipe banging has stopped. The only sounds are of running water and the countryside.

I have a piss and then decide that the tank is full enough and shut the water off. I heave the container out to the van. I was right – it's far too heavy to have carried it any further.

Remembering the showerhead I have left on the hand basin, I return. For some reason it won't go back on straight. Screwing it back onto the tube is a ridiculously simple task, but it just won't go.

I curse and unscrew it and start again, and again. And again! Every time it cross-threads and gets stuck, so I return to the van and hunt out a pair of pliers. As I fiddle, trying to force the damned tube to screw onto the stupid showerhead, I frown at something – at a thought slowly surfacing even though my brain is occupied with the task at hand.

Finally with a little brute force, the nut slips into alignment and tightens satisfyingly. I breathe a sigh of relief and just at that second I realise what is bothering me.

The banging in the pipes has started again. *And there's no water running.*

I turn to head out into the daylight, and then pause and suck on my bottom lip and listen for a moment to the regular clanging sound.

I tap the cold water pipe with the pliers to see if it makes the same sound, to see if that's where the noise comes from. It makes an identical echoing tap-tap-tap sound. *"Maybe that's why they call them taps,"* I think.

And then a really strange thing happens. The pipes reply. I smile and raise an eyebrow at the spookiness of Dante's intelligent plumbing, and tap the pipe again, three times this time.

As I turn to leave, again there's a reply. *Clang, clang, clang.*

My pulse increases a little. My smile fades.

Then I get it. Laughing, I dump the pliers in the washbasin and jog around to the front of the house, knowing that I will find the front door open; knowing that Tom is in the kitchen tapping out messages at the kitchen sink and grinning at me.

But it's locked. There's still no one home.

I check the windows, but they too are locked. I check the side window – the shutters are closed. I run around to the back of the house, to what I figure must be Dante's bedroom window, but the shutters are closed there as well.

Dante's place usually looks like a bomb just went off inside, with all the windows and doors blown outwards. I have never seen everything look so closed.

I bash the faded green louvers of the shutter with my fist and try to think what to do next.

I hear the noise again, though fainter here, less metallic, more deadened than before. It's also closer, clearly coming from behind the shutters.

"Think," I say out loud. *Doorlocks, windows, pipes, shutters. Shutters!*

I had shutters like these when I lived in Grasse. Now if they're just the same...

I run to the front of the house and grab a rusting bar of metal; then I jog back and peer through between the louvered slats.

I force the bar into place. If I'm right, then there's a retaining clip, somewhere... *here*! The bar pops up with a clang. "*Yes*," I exclaim as I swing the shutters open.

Yellow Provencal curtains glare back at me. I run back to the front of the house and grab an empty crate.

With it propped against the wall I can just see through the tiny gap at the top where the curtains meet. I lift a hand to shade my eyes from the sunlight.

Everything is vague and yellow in the filtered light. I make out Dante's bed, unmade but empty. I lean to the left and on the right-hand side of the room I can see a chair covered in clothes.

I hear the banging again, so I lean to the right to try and check out the other side, but I lose my balance and have to jump down.

"What if they come home," I think. *"How are you going to explain climbing crates, peering through gaps in curtains?"*

I move the crate to the right, and climb up again. Now I can see the bookcase on the left-hand wall and the radiator. And at the base of the radiator, a shape – a pile of sheets, no, a blanket... I cup my hands and strain to see but it's so hard – the sun is right against the side of my face.

And then the thing moves. It jumps and jerks, and as it does so it makes the clanking noise. For an instant I think it's...

"Dante*!*" I mutter, ducking out of sight.

But my shadow is all over the window. My silhouette is printed across the curtains like a big *Mark was here* sign. So I straighten, take a deep breath and brazenly knock on the window.

"Is anyone in *there*?" I shout.

The clanking repeats, but there is no other reply, so I peer in again.

It takes a while for my eyes to readjust, but this time I make out a profile – a head. There *is* someone in there; I can see him now, straining and trying to turn to face me. I blink hard and lean further. I bash my forehead hard against the window.

At the sound or maybe at the sight of me, the shape becomes frantic, jerking around in a mad clanking bundle.

I chew the inside of my mouth. I'm not quite sure what I'm seeing yet, but it's fucked up. It's not a normal thing.

"*Hello*?" I shout. "If you can hear me..."

My voice fades away. The shape, a jerking, jumping mess, moves strangely, like a cat in a sack, or a tethered pig or...

And only then do I get it.

It has taken *far* longer than it should have for me to understand what I'm seeing. As it finally dawns on me, my words are just the sound of my breath.

"*Oh God!*" I whisper.

With my mouth still open in awe, I whack the flat of my hand against the window, and jump down from the crate.

I grab a soil-coated brick, and making a guess at the height of the clasp, I shield my eyes and smash the corresponding pane of glass. In the silence of mid-day, the sound of the falling glass is out of all proportion to the size of the pane I have broken. I knock the jagged corners away, and carefully reach through to release the lock.

The two halves of the window swing inwards, straining against the curtains. Sunlight streams into the room.

I jump down, crunching on the fallen glass. The room smells fetid, almost sewer-like. I pull the curtains fully open, and I turn nervously to the left.

Though I brace myself for it, the reality of the vision that confronts me still takes my breath away.

He looks up at me, his eyes sad, dog-like. His cheeks are glistening with tears. I shake my head, momentarily unable to believe my eyes.

His ankles and hands are chained to the base of the radiator; silver gaffer tape covers his mouth. He's entirely naked.

I move to his side and start to clumsily fiddle with the tape around his head. Tears are welling up, blurring my vision.

"Tom," I say gently. "What on earth…" I can see the spasms of Tom's distraught breathing and he nods, eyes wide, egging me on. I wince and pull at the tape – it's stuck to his hair, to his skin, to his ears. With a yank, I rip it from his face.

He gulps for air. He sounds like he's hyperventilating. "My nose," he pants. "It's blocked… I couldn't breathe."

I finger the handcuffs restraining him and sigh desperately. "Who did this?" I say. "*Dante?*"

"Be quick," Tom says, his voice cracking. "Please, get me out of here before they get back."

"But how did you…?"

"Later," Tom begs. "*Please?*"

I wipe the tears from my eyes and stare at the metal handcuffs. "Sure babe," I say. "But how? There's an axe out front, could I bust them?"

Tom shakes his head. "They're Paolo's, I think they're strong," he says.

The smell is overpowering and I gag and have to turn away for an instant, then I lean back over Tom's trembling body and finger the chains.

"Yeah, they need a bolt cutter or something," I say.

Tom starts to shiver. He looks like he's losing it.

"Tom, don't," I say, my voice uneven. "I'll fix it."

"But if they get back…" Tom says.

"They?" I say. "What about the key, did you see what they did with the key?"

Tom shakes his head.

"Fuck," I breathe.

"I could call the pol…" I shake my head. "These are Paolo's, right?"

Tom nods and desperately twists his wrists. I notice that they are starting to bleed. I finger the handcuffs and look skyward. *"Please,"* I think. *"Just one idea."*

The second I look back down at the radiator, it's obvious. "I know Tom," I say. "Don't move."

Despite everything, Tom manages to roll his eyes at the crassness of the statement.

The bedroom door is locked, so I climb back out through the window and run round to the van for a pipe wrench.

The nuts at the base of the radiator have fifty years' paint on them and it's impossible to get a grip. I open the wrench and position it again, and again. My shaking hands aren't helping either.

"Oh, come *on*," Tom whispers.

"It will work," I tell him. I look up at the ceiling again. "It will work!" I insist.

And suddenly the nut moves. Only a millimetre or so, but it moves. Tom sees it. "Yes!" he says.

I can only get about a quarter of a turn before I have to reposition the wrench, so progress is terrifyingly slow, but water starts to drip from the base of the radiator. As I manage another half-turn it turns to a trickle, and finally, in a gurgling gush of rusty water, the nut spins free.

I sit in the puddle, and brace one foot against the wall, ready to struggle with the pipe but it's lead and bends easily away.

Tom slides the bracelets over the end. His right foot and hand still have handcuffs on them, but the ends now dangle free.

He moves onto one knee. "My leg's gone to sleep," he says, stretching his arm and then using his mouth to move the bracelet away from the red welt on his wrist.

"God that smell," I say, screwing up my face. "What *is* that?"

Tom looks up at me. It's not just that he's forced to sit on the floor – he looks smaller than usual; he looks as though he has shrunk.

"I shit myself," he says quietly.

My eyes flick downwards and see that it's true. "Jesus," I say.

I don't know what's going on here, but with such an undeniable proof of Tom's terror, with such convincing evidence of imminent danger, I too start to tremble.

And the second nut won't budge at all. "Fucking, bloody, plumbing!" I gasp as I heave on the wrench.

Every time it slips the nut becomes a little more rounded. Every time the wrench spins off and hits the wall, it becomes a little more impossible to undo.

I throw the wrench down and look around the room in search of inspiration. Tom has started to shiver again. "You mustn't let them catch you here..." he says quietly.

"Tom!" I say. "I can do it, just hang on..."

"Yeah, but if you can't... you mustn't let them catch you here."

"Shut it Tom!" I say. "Just let me think here."

"Lead pipes," I mutter.

I jump up and position my feet squarely in front of the radiator. I grasp the two top corners, brace myself, and pull.

In fact the radiator is just resting on the wall bracket. It slides easily towards me, too easily. It's so heavy I nearly fall over in surprise.

"Cast iron..." I say breathily, laying the free corner on the flagstones.

I start to slide it back and forth.

"What the fuck are you doing?" Tom asks. "You don't think it's gonna *snap* do you?"

It scrapes and screams against the floor as I push it forwards, then tug it backwards.

"It's lead," I say.

"It's just bending," Tom says.

"It's lead, it'll snap eventually. It's soft."

"Can't we cut it?" Tom says. "Can't we cut it with the axe?"

"Yes!" I say. "Yes, that'll work."

I vault back out the window and run to the front of the house, grab the axe and sprint back.

"Okay, get as far back as you can," I say, positioning my back to the wall, and raising the axe. A bead of sweat stings my eye.

It cuts through the lead pipe like a knife through butter. It's incredible. The remaining water spews out. Tom reaches with his free hand and twists the pipe forward releasing the ends of the second two sets of handcuffs.

He jumps to his feet, but then wobbles and collapses back against Dante's bed. "My legs are fucked," he says.

I hook his arm over my shoulder and help him onto a chair and out of the window, and then round the side of the house. We look like a shot from a war zone. We look like something from Guantanamo Bay.

"Put me in the back," Tom shouts, reaching for the door, a swinging handcuff banging against the side of the van.

I help him in, and slam the door then run to the front. I start the engine, and with one glance back at Tom – he's on all fours on the floor behind me – I rev the engine and start to move forwards.

"So I just drive, yeah?" I say.

"Yeah, be quick about it," Tom spits. "If we bump into them on the track we're dead."

The van lurches through the ruts and out of the gate. I can see the entrance to the lane in the distance.

"Faster," Tom says, peering over my shoulder.

"I'll break the axles if I go faster," I say.

At the end of the track, I hesitate.

"Left!" Tom shouts behind me.

"Home is right though," I say.

"LEFT!" he shouts.

I slam my foot to the floor. The van lurches out onto the main road. "Where are we going?"

"They'll think we've gone right," Tom says.

"Okay, but where are we going?" I say.

Tom doesn't answer. The air cooled engine of the van resounds and bounces against the hillside as I thrash it through the gears.

"Discreet getaway car," Tom says.

"Yeah," I say. "*Orange* too!"

As I round the corner a moped looms – I almost run into it. The fat rider has cages of chickens haphazardly piled and strapped across his luggage rack.

"Overtake," Tom says.

"Tom!" I shout. "Look at the road, will you? I *can't*."

Tom looks behind him. "Overtake!" he says. "Do it!"

"It's a blind bend," I say. "We'll die."

"We'll die if you *don't*," Tom says solemnly.

I swallow and ram the gearbox into second. The engine roars like a biplane. "Here goes," I say. "Pray."

But just at the instant I start to put my foot down, just at the moment the van lurches towards the other lane, the farmer, terrified by the noise of the huge orange van, pulls over onto the hard shoulder.

The VW thunders past him, round the corner, up a hill, down to the next town, and then up again into the hills.

I glance back at Tom. He's cleaning himself with a beach-towel. He looks up at me pale faced. "Dante said that hole is my grave," he says.

His voice is so quiet I doubt what I have heard. "What hole?"

Tom shakes his head. "The one at the bottom of the garden," Tom says. "I thought it was a joke."

I shake my head. There's so much I can't figure out; I'm not even beginning to understand what has happened here. I don't even know where to start.

I glance back at Tom who is alternating between peering out the rear window and inspecting his foot. "Fucking glass in my foot too," he says. He sounds amazingly together. "Can't this thing go any faster?" he adds.

I shake my head. "Not round these bends," I say. "Not without rolling."

"I wish I had a gun," he says.

I frown. "Tom, what *exactly* are we running away from?"

I swing around a roundabout a little fast and the van tyres screech, and I'm aware of Tom stumbling against the bench seat. As the road straightens I glance back at him in the rear-view mirror. He's pulling a blanket around himself.

"I don't understand what's happened here," I say. More to the point I don't understand how the Tom that I know, that I *thought I knew*, could get to this point. It makes no sense to me.

Tom runs a hand across his mouth, the handcuff dangling. "Later," he says.

I turn and look back at him. "What do you mean *later*?"

"I don't really know," he says, his voice aquiver. "I don't know what to say."

"That's not enough," I say. "I need to know what's..."

"Dante and Paolo... They're in it together."

"In *what* together?"

"I don't know!" Tom shouts. "Jesus, Mark! The road!" he shrieks.

I jerk my head back to face the road, and inelegantly correct our lane position.

"I just heard random words," Tom continues.

I sigh and shake my head. "*What* words?" I say, my irritation leaking out. "And which way here? Motorway?"

"Yeah, the Autostrada and then north," Tom says. "They'll never expect that."

"But don't you want to get back to France?" I say. "Wouldn't we be safer in France?"

"Not yet," Tom says. "GO!"

I point the van towards the Autostrada, and slam my foot to the floor. "You overheard what?" I ask again.

Tom moves forward and leans on the back of my seat. "They said, *uccidete quello per prima*," he says quietly. "It means *kill that one first.*"

I glance at him and look back at the road.

"*Uccidete quello per prima,*" he repeats. "Kill that one first..."

As we pound along the Italian Autostrada, the relief of putting physical distance between ourselves and the danger – known and unknown, stated and still unsaid – is ecstatic. For a while it feels obvious that this is just a reprieve, that in a glimpse of a mirror or the wail of a siren, our escape will be over, that our hunters – whoever they are and whatever they want – will catch up with us. But as time goes by, as the minutes and kilometres pass, my brain starts to accept the idea that it is *just* possible that this is where the chapter ends.

Tom is silent and watchful, but an hour into the journey when I see that he has stopped watching the traffic through the rear window, I realise that he too is adjusting to the possibility of escape.

The only conversation between us happens near a town called Pontrenolli, when I try again to convince Tom that we should swing homeward. His response is hysterical, and in deference to his justifiably jangled nerves more than any feeling that he may be right (I am actually convinced that he is wrong), I shut up and continue northwards.

Just after six, as the heat of the day starts to fade, I come to a major fork and have to decide whether to head west towards Alessandria or still further north to Milano.

I ask Tom what to do, but when no response comes I frown and glance behind me. He's fast asleep, nestled, despite the temperature, in a mound of sleeping bags.

As I approach the point where the motorways split, the sight of a police car on the hard shoulder makes me shiver. How on earth would we explain Tom's police issue handcuffs to an Italian officer, I wonder.

I quickly compute two possible futures. Staying in Italy involves finding a hotel, smuggling a chained Tom in, or sleeping with him – unwashed – in the van. It involves the constant stress that someone will notice something, that the police will pull us over, that a man on a campsite or in a hotel lobby will phone the cops, and what would *that* entail? And it means yours truly is going to have to find cutting or grinding equipment in Italian, in Italy in order to deal with the handcuffs.

Heading back, on the other hand, merely involves ignoring Tom's will, maybe arguing with him about the risks when/if he awakens, and ultimately taking responsibility for my decision if something goes wrong.

I glance at the road atlas on the seat beside me and I glimpse the name Cuneo, on the map.

Cuneo, where I once went with the bike club. Cuneo, up over the mountains, over the beautiful hairpin bends of the *Arriere Pays Nicoise*. With the realisation that I know a route over the mountains that neither Dante nor Paolo could ever hope to think of, my hesitation is over. With a half-guilty glance at Tom, I push my foot back to the floor and head west.

Tom sleeps like a man who has been drugged – the adrenalin comedown I presume. Occasionally I can even hear him snoring over the sound of the engine. Thankfully though he stirs, he never wakens, so we thunder west past Alessandra, then on past Alba, and then on around Cuneo and finally up towards the range of the southern Alps separating Italy from home.

I'm shattered myself – my eyes feel as though they have been flattened with a hammer and polished, maybe with grit – but I know that once I get into the hills the road will be familiar; I know that I can do this.

My mind wanders and I wonder if Tom will be angry when he wakes up, and then I wonder if the trauma of this event will leave any sequel on him, on us, on me.

And there is of course the question still lingering, still hanging over us. The great, unasked interrogation that needs to be answered before any of us can move on.

The thought makes me so angry, my vision tints red, so I squeeze it away by wondering what we can eat when we get home, and how nice it will be to see Jenny and Paloma. Strangely the thought of the cat is so emblematic that it makes me want to weep, so I push that thought away too, this time by trying to remember who was with me the last time I rode these bends. I squint against the sun setting in the rear-view mirror, and realise that the bends are going to become ever more treacherous with the end of daylight.

We're nearing the top of the huge Col de Tende, the border within spitting distance when, his mouth mere inches from my ear, Tom suddenly says, "Jesus! Where the fuck are we?"

I jolt in surprise. "I thought you were asleep," I say.

"Yeah," Tom yawns, "I was." He leans forward and peers out at the stretch of winding road lit by the van's headlights. "So where *are* we?"

I turn and give him a cocky wink. "Wait," I say. "Ten seconds, there's a sign round the next bend. It's a surprise."

Tom rubs his eyes and leans still further forward. Even though he has towelled himself off there's a fruity smell about him that's not entirely pleasant. I wrinkle my nose, and watch for the signpost.

When it first comes into view, it's a vague blue square, but as the van rounds the bend, as the headlamps fall upon it, it glows astonishingly bright, a beacon of hope in the deep dark night. The white lettering – *France* – is almost blinding, the sign – *Département des Alpes Maritimes* – almost tear-jerkingly beautiful.

"Oh," Tom says.

I brace myself for an argument, or congratulations, but neither are forthcoming. Tom simply slumps back into the rear seat.

I frown to myself, my anger mounting. I shoot a puzzled glare back at him. "The mountain route," I say, in case he hasn't quite understood. "Home in about 2 hours."

Tom stares at me, and shrugs. I can see his eyes, deep and glassy in the mirror, but still he says nothing, so I shrug and drive on, ever more furious.

A few minutes have passed before he finally manages to respond, and it's only then that I realise that he has been too choked to reply.

"Thanks," he says, his voice cracked and raw with emotion.

I nod slowly. "You're welcome," I say.

"I don't deserve you," he adds in a broken whisper.

I swallow hard, and chew the inside of my mouth. There, again is the great unspoken question. I wrench the wheel around another bend.

When I swing into the car park three full hours later, not a single word has been spoken.

Tom silently tucks the loose ends of his chains into his socks and the sleeves of his jacket and shambles from the van.

I'm having trouble looking him in the eye, scared of what I might find. But I needn't worry, for, as I lock the doors and finally force myself to look at him, he averts his own gaze and stares at his feet.

The flat looks dead and alien, seemingly bearing little relationship to whoever we have become over the past few days.

I almost desperately want to see Paloma, but I don't want to speak to Jenny yet, not till I know what I am saying. So the cat will have to stay upstairs for now.

While Tom clankingly showers I cook pasta, open a tin of tuna, serve up two portions, and wolf down my half. Then, while Tom eats, I shower. His chains – I note absent-mindedly – have scratched the bath.

We end up side by side, not touching, still not having spoken a word. It's a bad sign, and it makes me hesitate as I wonder whether I'm really ready for the whole story.

"Goodnight," I say, my courage momentarily deserting me.

"Goodnight," Tom says.

We lie like this, side by side, suddenly strangers. I stare at the ceiling for a minute or two until I realise that there will be no sleep until it's dealt with, and maybe no sleep even then. But just as I open my mouth to speak, it's Tom that says my name.

"Mark?"

"Yes?"

"You *will* be able to get these off tomorrow, won't you?"

Even though Tom can't see me, I nod in the darkness. "Yeah," I say. "I'll get a grinder from Castorama tomorrow. It'll be a bit scary, but it shouldn't be too difficult."

"Thanks," Tom says. "Goodnight then."

The bed bounces as he rolls away.

"Tom?" I say.

"Um?"

"I have to ask this. I'm sorry, but it won't go away. I... I feel like I don't know you anymore."

"Umm?" Tom asks, his voice suddenly sleepy.

"Well..." I suddenly don't know where to start.

I can hear Tom is holding his breath.

"The thing is..." I say. "I mean... Well..."

Tom makes a tutting noise and exhales. "What?" he asks. "What is it?"

His irritated tone spurs me on. "Okay," I say. "How *exactly* did you come to be naked and chained to a radiator?"

"You know," he mumbles. "Dante did it."

"Sure," I say. "But *how* did he do it? How did he get you into that position?"

"Tomorrow," Tom says.

I frown and chew my bottom lip. Tom makes a vague snoring noise.

Then I cough and say, as gently as I can manage, "Feigning sleep won't cut it you know."

A moment passes, maybe a minute, maybe two. The bed jerks and wobbles beside me, and then Tom gulps and his voice quivers beside me, mumbling through tears. "I, erm," he says. "I don't know what to say."

I raise a hand to cover my mouth and force my eyes closed against my own tears as he says, "I'm sorry; I'm really sorry."

What It Takes To Forgive

I close the door quietly, and step into the lounge.

Jenny peeks her head out of the kitchenette and nods me towards the dining room.

"She's just gone down," she murmurs. "Dinner's ready, so sit down and I'll bring it through."

I sit on the sofa bed and wince at the creak of the springs. I look around the room at the slow changes – the African rugs, the plants, the books – which are slowly turning this anonymous flat into Jenny's place, and now – with the addition of teddy bears and rattles – into Jenny and Sarah's.

Jenny appears in the doorway, a steaming saucepan of cheesy pasta in one hand and a serving fork in the other. "It's pretty basic I'm afraid," she says, plonking the pan on the coffee table and pulling up a pouf.

She shuffles closer to the table, and then closes her eyes and sighs, visibly trying to relax. When she opens them again, she looks at me as if she has just seen me for the first time and smiles. "Open that wine would you?" she says. "I'm gasping."

I slide the bottle of Bordeaux towards me and reach for the corkscrew. "So is this motherhood lark wearing you out?" I ask. The cork pops from the bottle as Jenny drops the first ladleful of pasta onto my plate.

"Not really," she replies, then more thoughtfully, "In a way, I suppose."

I smile vaguely and fill our glasses. "Make up your mind," I say lightly.

Jenny shrugs and shakes her head. "It's fine really," she says. "It doesn't take a lot of brainpower, bringing up a baby. Or even much physical effort really…"

I raise my glass and Jenny pulls a face and blows through her lips and we clink our glasses together. "It's just sort of…" her voice fades away and she shakes her head dreamily.

"Relentless?" I say.

She nods. "Yeah," she says. "Relentless covers it. You're just, you know, occupied all the time… in a sort of droning low level way. It's numbing really, that's all."

I frown and taste the pasta for the first time. It's overcooked but the sauce is rich with cheese and cream. "No regrets though?" I ask in a concerned tone.

Jenny laughs and shakes her head. "No!" she laughs. "She's the most wonderful thing that ever happened to me," then, "I guess that sounds contradictory." She rolls tagliatelli around her fork and raises it to her mouth, but pauses and adds, "Anyway, enough of me; how are *you*?"

I swallow my food and shrug. "I'm Okay I guess," I say.

She shakes her head. "You're *so* not!" she laughs.

I snort dismissively and smile at her. "Don't ask then," I say. "If you know the answer."

"Have you at least *spoken* to him yet?" she says.

I raise an eyebrow. "*Tom*?" I ask.

Jenny rolls her eyes at me. "I don't believe you sometimes," she says.

I stare at my wineglass for a moment, running my finger through the mist that has formed. "It's not *my* fault," I say eventually. "I mean – I'm not the one that fucked it all up."

"Yeah, but you are the one that's not forgiving," Jenny says.

I shrug. "Forgiving *what* though?" I say. "Forgiving who? I mean, I'm not sure I know who Tom is anymore."

Jenny shrugs and sighs.

"You know he never even told me what happened. He just packed his bags and ran away."

"He was ashamed," Jenny says. "When we were cutting those things off, well, he couldn't even look *me* in the eye."

I nod. "I know that," I say with a sigh. "I understand that. But it's hard you know. When you don't even know what you're supposed to be forgiving. Or how it happened."

Jenny nods slowly. "I guess," she says. "But if it's making you unhappy, well... Maybe you need to get it all clear, even if it's just for yourself."

I nod and swallow hard. "And there's the question of trust," I say. "I mean, when I think about talking to Tom and sorting things out I kind of think, you know – what's the point? I think it would be hard to trust him again... After that."

Jenny sighs and looks me in the eye. Her eyes are deep pools of sympathy.

"Hey," I say with forced cheer. "Can we talk about you again? It's much more fun..."

It's only just eleven when I get back to my flat - Jenny goes to bed early these days. I sit and think about Tom. Again. As if by sitting and thinking some mysterious key will appear, spontaneously, in my mind; something that would make me understand – and maybe love – this man again. But, as always, the magical key eludes me.

It's true, of course, what Jenny says. I haven't smiled properly since Tom left. And sooner or later he and I *will* have to talk. The story between us clearly isn't finished yet.

Maybe it does just need a phone call to finish everything once and for all. Maybe that really *is* all I need to do so that I can move on. Maybe that's exactly why I'm *not* phoning.

I glance at the phone. Tom's number is still programmed into quick-dial #1. I lift the receiver and sigh. I run a fingernail along the crack where the plastic joins.

Maybe I should phone him. I could say... But it's been nearly three months. *What* could I say?

I lay the receiver back on the base, and – feeling slightly sick – I head for the bathroom and bed.

August is a dead month in France. It's too hot to breathe down here in the south, and half the country is on holiday whilst the other half stays behind to man the phones. They don't ring much, of course, so I have time to think about Tom. Too much time really.

Every few hours an email appears in the list before me, and I lazily click on it and answer a question or send back a price list.

It's dull as ditchwater, but to be honest it's about all my brain can handle. It's been hard going back to work after such a long break, and my guess – that it would be a gentle way of easing myself back into the world of work – has turned out to be right

It's hard to believe that this repetitive, eventless unfolding of each day can fit into the same life as the mad adventures of the last few months, but… I look across the room. Through the door I can see the secretary playing solitaire on her computer. My eyes tell me that this truly *is* all that is happening.

So I have lots of time to think. Plenty of time to wonder who Dante really is; what he and Paolo really get up to. I have time to wonder how Tom is doing, to tell myself that I don't care anymore, and even enough time to realise that that's not true. By 7 PM when I get home, this single Monday in August seems to have lasted longer than the whole of June.

I throw my bag onto the sofa; stroke Paloma who stretches and screeches in a unique way that lets me know she's not keen on me going out to work all day either.

The red light on my answer phone is winking at me, so I hit play and sit, strangely unsurprised, as Tom's voice hesitantly stumbles from the tinny speaker. Then I pour a stiff whisky and call him back. He answers immediately.

The brightness in his voice, the feigned surprise at my call makes me think that this isn't going to be the easy, honest communication I was hoping for. I close my eyes.

"It's good to hear your voice," Tom says.

I nod slowly and bite my bottom lip.

"Mark?" he says.

I swallow and clear my throat, which seems, suddenly, to be coated with phlegm. "Yeah," I say. "It's been a long time."

"I'm sorry about that," Tom says.

"I roll my head from side to side and stretch my neck muscles. "You called eventually," I say. "Well done for that… at least."

"Yeah…" Tom says thoughtfully. "I wasn't sure you'd want to speak to me."

"Do I?" I wonder. Pressure is building behind my eyes. All of the hurt of the last three months is resurfacing, not only because of what happened in Italy, but the hurt of his leaving, and now the hurt of it taking *three months* for him to call me.

"So why now?" I croak.

There's a pause before Tom answers. "I don't really know," he says.

We sit in silence for a moment. I nod thoughtfully, breathing with difficulty.

Tom coughs at the other end of the line. "I haven't seen you online," he says after a while.

"My computer crashed," I say. "I lost all my contacts." It's a lie of course. I have a Mac – it never crashes. I deleted Tom from my MSN the day he left.

"Oh," he says.

I shake my head as if to dislodge the feeling of fuzziness building in my brain. "So did you want something specific?" I say, realising that someone is going to have to force something to happen, and then, that this sounded harsh.

"Yeah…" Tom says vaguely. "I really just wanted to hear your voice."

I nod. "Okay," I say.

"And I had some good news. I thought I should tell you," he adds.

I nod. I was thinking apologies more than good news. "Yeah?" I say.

"I got my, erm, results," Tom says. "My test results."

I frown. "Your *results*," I repeat.

"Yeah," Tom laughs falsely. "I'm still negative thank god."

I stop breathing. I pinch the bridge of my nose.

"I thought you should know," he continues. "I had to wait three months to be sure."

I can't think of a reply. I sit silently, my mouth open; I consider hanging up.

"You still there?" Tom asks.

I exhale hard. "Yeah," I say. "Just about."

"Just about?" Tom says.

"I didn't know," I say. "I didn't know that you *needed* to do a test."

"*No*..." Tom says. "Well... I was worried. I didn't know his status, and, well, especially after his comments about Aids not really existing and all that," Tom says.

"His status..." I repeat weakly.

"Dante's," Tom says.

I swallow and scrunch my eyes against the tears. "I didn't know what you did," I say. "I still *don't* know what you did. You never said."

"Well, you imagined though," Tom says defensively.

"I didn't know you had sex though," I say. "I didn't know you let that... I didn't know you let him fuck you without a condom."

Tom sighs unhappily. "I really miss you," he says, his voice wobbling.

I screw up my eyes. "That's not really good enough," I say. "You can't just phone me and tell me... You can't just tell me stuff like that and expect..."

"I didn't *let* him do anything," Tom breathes. "You know that much at least."

I shake my head. My tears are fading, the hurt is turning to anger. "I know what you tell me," I say, my voice measured. "And it's not much."

"I know."

"But even that's too much."

Tom says nothing.

"And you did let him do something," I say. "As I understand it, you let Dante undress you and handcuff you."

Silence.

"When did you *actually* say 'no' Tom?"

Tom sighs again. "Do we really have to go through all that?" he asks.

I shake my head. "*This is pointless,*" I think.

The phone sounds muffled, and I can hear that Tom is crying. I rub a hand through my hair. "*No* Tom," I say. "We don't have to go through anything. We don't have to go through anything at all." I wait for a moment, and then add, "I think I'm going to hang up Tom. I can't really see the point..."

I wait for him to reply but the line clicks dead instead.

I cover my head with my suit jacket but the outrageously heavy October rain soaks it immediately, dripping through the fabric and running down my neck, lashing horizontally at my legs, soaking my feet. I run in from the deluge and squelch up the stairs where I push into my apartment with a gasp, slamming the door behind me.

I pull off my shirt and grab a towel from the bathroom to dry my hair, but even before I do that my phone rings – it's Jenny.

"You should come upstairs," she says. "I have something for you."

"I'll just change," I tell her. "I'm soaked. What is it anyway?"

"Huh," she says mysteriously. "*It* is a surprise."

She opens the door grinning broadly. I frown at her and then kiss her on the cheek. "What's up with you then?" I ask.

"I found something on your doormat," she says, nodding towards the lounge. "In there."

Only then do I see him on the sofa. My bemused smile slips away. "*Hugo?*" I say.

Hugo has his hands clasped between his knees. He looks up at me and grins. "*Grande surprise hein?*" he says.

I nod. "Yeah…" I say vaguely. "*Big* surprise."

Jenny nudges me forwards, and as I stumble into the lounge Hugo stands and moves around the coffee table to kiss me hello.

"So how come you never mentioned *this* one before," Jenny murmurs saucily.

"I was passing through, so I thought I'd come say hi," Hugo says. "For old time's sake."

"He was sitting on your doormat," Jenny tells me. "I thought with the rain and stuff…"

"Yeah," I say. "Thanks, um…" I suck my teeth and frown. "I'm sorry Jenny," I say. "But I need to um…" I start to lead Hugo towards the door. "I need to talk to Hugo alone really."

Jenny winks at me as if she knows what I mean. "I bet you do," she says.

Hugo, clearly embarrassed, waves at Jenny as I push him out onto the landing. "Oh… My bag," he says.

I reach for the bag beside the door, and as I turn to leave, Jenny says, quietly, "He's lovely."

I laugh dryly. "*Yeah,*" I say. "*Right.*"

"What the hell are you doing here?" I demand, pushing the door to my apartment closed.

Hugo shrugs. "I said. I was passing through…"

Paloma stretches and screeches. Hugo strokes her comfortably, naturally, easily. It strikes me, perhaps unfairly, that the gesture is a claiming of territory; it's as if he has never been away.

"How did you even get my address? I mean it's been…" I push my lips out and shake my head.

"Three years?" Hugo says.

I nod. "Yeah, three years, without a word…"

Hugo frowns lopsidedly and steps forward, releasing the handle of his bag.

"Hey, slow down," he says. "Relax." He grabs my elbows. His hands are warm. The contact feels good.

I stand paralysed waiting for my brain to tell me how to react, but it's as if I have done a Google search and it's come up empty. Your search – "how to behave with an ex who dumped me for no reason and who is back and leaning towards me for a kiss," – did not match *any* documents.

I shake my head jerkily. "This is just… *unexpected*," I say.

Hugo's thumbs are caressing my elbows. He leans in and hugs me. "Relax," he says. "You don't have to do anything, just let yourself be surprised. It's a *good* surprise isn't it?"

Hugo smells the same as he always did, and that smell, his sweet musky odour, is like a time machine, linking the distant past, the time we were together, with here and now.

He pulls back a little and stares deep into my eyes and grins, then leans forward and rubs the tip of his nose against mine, Eskimo style.

In my mind I say something Gloria-Gaynor-like, maybe, *"Hey don't get cute. Don't think you can behave like a complete cunt and then waltz back in here. Just turn around and…"* I hover between collapsing into anger or tears, and then, almost despite myself, what I *actually* do is kiss him. Hugo laughs lightly and kisses me back. My body goes limp.

Hugo helps me prepare dinner. It's bizarre how naturally we slip back into our roles, into our easy navigation around each other. As I chop veg he leans into my back and slides his hands into my pockets. He nuzzles my neck.

We gulp down a couple of martini's each – I think we both need it – and then open a bottle of dry white to drink with the meal. Halfway through the bottle we are chatting comfortably, easily avoiding the unspeakable subject of our break-up.

The second Hugo has finished eating he grabs the sleeve of my t-shirt and pulls me through to the bedroom.

An internal dialogue is accusing me of being easy, of being a walkover, of letting myself be screwed by the bastard that is, undoubtedly, Hugo. But another part of me is more powerful. I haven't had sex for months and the contact with him is, *as always*, ecstatic. I *want* to get screwed here. It's *exactly* what I want.

Rediscovering his dancer's body is even better than the first time, and as I undress him my dick trembles and judders with anticipation. Everything about him is as I remember, from the soft down of his chest hair to his sticky out belly-button, to his porn-star dick.

We kiss and fumble and explore each other bodies. It's pure rapture. Then he rolls on top of me and rubs his nose against mine, and I remember what comes next. As his dick slips between my legs I break into a grin.

"I want to fuck you," he says.

"I know," I whisper.

"Condom?" he says.

I blink slowly and reach behind me.

In the morning I awaken first. For the shortest time I think that the body beside me is Tom. Then I remember that it's Hugo, and then doubt myself, and have to look and see that it really is.

I shuffle across the bed to his back. His skin is very different from Tom's – softer, warmer; it feels as if it's covered in talc.

I lie there in a moment of half sleep, simultaneously thrilled and mortified that this is Hugo, not Tom. It's an astonishing moment, because as I awaken, it suddenly becomes clear to me just how much I fancy Hugo. And just how much I love Tom.

For most of my life those two concepts, sex and love, have been confused, even to the point where, through my lust for Hugo, I believed that I loved him; even thought he was *the* love of my life. Yes, my lust for Hugo's body, for this contact with his skin is a whole different kind of pleasure to what I feel when I have sex with Tom. But it's nothing to do with love at all; it's something else entirely. Chemical, or biological, or hormonal, who knows?

Hugo stretches.

Hugo's betrayal: his failure to mention his wife, his child, his other lover Antonio, well, it's at least as profound as Tom's, and yet here I am sleeping with him. And the reason that it doesn't matter isn't the passage of time. It's simply that I don't love Hugo. Maybe I never did.

I love Tom.

Hugo responds to my touch and yawns and stretches back towards me. "I didn't know where I was for a minute," he says.

I smile, a strange contented feeling enveloping me, and I roll onto my back. I feel as if I have just aged, as if in this particular moment I have become a different, older, wiser person. There are moments like that when you suddenly notice that you are different. And then the moment is forgotten, and you carry on with life, completely unaware of the change.

Hugo yawns and sits up. "What time is it?" he asks blearily.

I roll and reach for the alarm clock. "Nearly half nine," I tell him.

"*Merde!*" Hugo exclaims, sliding to the side of the bed. "I have to go," he says. "I have to be in Bordeaux by tonight."

I smile. I don't know quite why I'm smiling, whether it's because I'm not surprised at his sudden, tactless departure, or at the fact that I don't care.

"Shall I get up and make coffee or something," I ask. I know the answer already, but never let it be said that *I* was the rude one.

"No," Hugo says, hopping into his jeans. "No, I'm really sorry, but I have to go. I have so much to do."

To hide my grin I feign a yawn and cover my mouth, and watch as Hugo pulls on his t-shirt.

I lie in bed, stroking Paloma and listening to the sound of Hugo's mad rush around the apartment. Finally he pokes his head around the door.

"Sorry," he says.

I shrug and shake my head. "It's fine."

"Thanks," Hugo says with a snort. "You've been cool."

I nod slowly. "Haven't I?" I agree.

"But I have to…" Hugo nods behind him towards the door.

I nod. "Get back to your wife?" I say.

Hugo pales. His features slip into a frown. He didn't know that I knew about his massive deception.

I smile, "It's fine," I say. "Go!"

Hugo opens his mouth to speak, and then closes it again. He shakes his head quickly and then raises the palm of his hand. I'm not sure if it's a gesture of surrender or a goodbye wave.

"Ciao!" He says.

I get up late – just before 12. The sight of sunshine is such a relief after yesterday's rain. I dress quickly.

As I lock the door to my flat, I hear Jenny upstairs, doing the same, so I wait until she reaches my landing.

"Hello!" I say. "I'm sorry about yesterday."

Jenny grins at me and wiggles Sarah's hand at me. "Say hello to Mark," she urges. Sarah gurgles happily. "It's fine," Jenny tells me. "I understand entirely. He's lovely."

I snort. "Yeah, well," I say, following her downstairs. "Not as lovely as you think. Not lovely at all in fact."

As I follow them down, Sarah peers at me over Jenny's shoulder, her head bobbing in rhythm with the steps. "Where are you off to?" Jenny asks.

"Just out for coffee," I say. "Making the most of the sun while it lasts."

Sarah makes an exclamatory, "*Goo!*" sound.

"Me too," Jenny says. "So you can tell me all about the lovely Hugo."

The daylight outside is stunningly bright. The atmosphere has been purged by the storms, and the UV rays – finding nothing in their path – shine piercingly down, prickling my skin. We settle in a nearby café on Place Rosetti and order two coffees before Jenny says, "So?"

I laugh. "I thought I'd got away with it," I say.

She shakes her head. "You're joking."

"You're turning into a real fag hag you know," I tell her.

She shrugs cutely, and repeats. "So?"

I laugh. "I got a nice shag."

Jenny nods as if she's moderately impressed.

"And then he left," I say, pulling an, *oh well* expression.

"Oh."

"Yeah. Back to his wife and child I expect."

Jenny's smile slips away. "Oh," she says again.

"He was already married when we dated. Only he never told me," I explain.

Jenny nods. "A *real* bisexual then?"

I shrug. "That's the big question isn't it?"

Jenny frowns so I continue, "Bisexuals are like UFOs," I say. "*Well*, do they exist or don't they?"

She tips her head sideways and sighs. "If he has a kid… Well, I take it you *know* how people make babies. *Right?*"

I laugh. "I guess," I say. "Just about."

Jenny wrinkles her nose. "Shame though," she says. "For you I mean." She turns to Sarah who is starting to writhe and fidget. "Do you want to sit with Mark, honey?" But as she lifts Sarah towards me she starts to scream – a short, sharp warning shot. Jenny pulls a face, and snuggles her back against her chest. "Sorry," she says.

"I have that effect on kids," I say. "And men apparently."

Sarah breaks into a smile and says, "*Angen.*"

"She's almost speaking," I say.

Jenny nods. "Yeah," she says. "She says *mum*, and *gat*."

I frown. "Gat?"

Jenny rolls her eyes. "Cat!" she says. "Doh! She loves Paloma though."

"Shame Paloma doesn't like her so much," I say. "She thinks Sarah is too shrieky by half."

The waiter brings coffee, and as he walks away Jenny sighs. I glance back at him and frown. "That's a big sigh," I say. "You in love with the cutey waiter or something?"

Jenny laughs. "Nah, I'm just disappointed for you," she says. "You deserve better luck. I thought maybe, well, you know…"

I wrinkle my nose. "I used to think I was in love with Hugo," I say. "I even used to think he was *the* love of my life."

Jenny strokes Sarah's hair and nods for me to continue.

"Turns out it was just sex," I say with a wry smile and a shrug.

Jenny laughs. "Funny how it takes so long to work these things out," she says. "I only just worked out that I really *did* love Nick."

I take a deep breath and look serious. "Don't you even think about…"

Jenny laughs and interrupts me. "Don't be daft," she says. "I'd never go back to him. I'm not *that* much of a masochist. I suppose I can identify the thing about him that I loved now though. It always seemed a bit of a mystery to me."

"As someone once pointed out to me, there's plenty of people we love, family, exes… But we can't live with them all," I say.

Jenny nods. "Yeah… And Tom?" she asks. "Talking of exes."

I blink slowly and cock my head to one side. "I expect I'll always love Tom," I say. "In one way or another."

Jenny nods and sips at her coffee. "In one way or another," she repeats.

"Well, I'll always love the Tom I knew. But maybe that was just a myth of Tom. Maybe the real Tom is the one who..." I shrug. "I really don't know."

"Do you think you'll see him again?"

I shrug. "I doubt it, he's had months to make a move; if he wanted to. My mythical Tom would have."

"I thought he phoned you," Jenny says.

I frown. I can't be sure but I don't remember telling Jenny about that. She shrugs and looks away – a little guiltily it strikes me.

"I thought that was what you said, anyway," Jenny says vaguely.

"Yeah," I say, still frowning at her in an accusatory fashion. "But if he wanted to patch things up, well, he hasn't exactly given it his best shot."

Jenny looks back at me and laughs lightly. "Is there really anything he *could* do?" she asks. "I mean, be honest."

I shrug. "People do. People explain. People write letters. People send flowers, People drop in... People drop to their knees and grovel," I say with a cynical laugh.

Jenny shrugs.

"You know what I mean though?" I say.

"Pretty hard for Tom to drop by," Jenny points out.

I nod. "Yeah," I say. "And *really* fucking hard to write a letter and apologise."

Jenny looks away again. "Maybe he thinks..."

But I can't hear her voice. I touch her arm. "I'm over here," I remind her.

"Sorry," she says, turning back. "I said, maybe he thinks it's pointless. Maybe he doesn't realise that you still care about him."

We stare each other out for a moment. Jenny raises an eyebrow. There's almost something confrontational about it. Then she shrugs. "I know how he feels about you, how he *felt* about you," she says. "That's all."

"Yeah," I nod. "He loved me *sooo* much – he decided to cheat on me, shag without a condom and run away. Oh and he thought it best never to actually explain himself or apologise. Nice one. Good strategy."

Jenny shrugs and jigs Sarah up and down. "Can you change your tone of voice a bit," she asks. "You're worrying her."

I look from Jenny to Sarah and see that her tiny brow is indeed furrowed, so I lean towards her and pull a face. "Hello you!" I say in a kiddie voice. "Everything's just fine, isn't it!" The frown slips away and her mouth slips into a tiny spittle-filled grin.

"Have *you* spoken to him?" I ask, as casually as I can.

Jenny frowns. "To Tom?"

I blink exaggeratedly. "Erm, *yeah*. To *Tom*."

She closes her eyes and shakes her head vigorously. "Of course not," she says. "I don't even have his number."

"So you wouldn't really know *what* he thinks, any more than I do," I point out raising an eyebrow. "*Right?*"

The postcard arrives on Wednesday. It's postmarked Monday morning. It says, "Hello from Brighton." It says, "I'm really sorry I fucked up," and it says, "I miss you." It could be a coincidence I figure. Just about.

The flowers arrive at work on Tuesday – a boxed bunch of wilting roses. Tom doesn't even know where I work, so there's definitely a mole in the house. I start to feel angry. It's not so much Jenny's breach of my trust, more Tom's lack of originality. I feel disingenuous for thinking it, but it seems to me that following Mark's three-step plan to forgiveness accurately transmitted by Jenny means absolutely nothing. It even seems to preclude any kind of genuine original gesture that Tom might have come up with himself.

I avoid Jenny all week – I really can't face rowing with her.

But the following Saturday when she knocks on my door, I'm ready for her. I set my jaw and grab the door handle. I must look pretty fierce because Tom's eyes widen. He bows his head and looks at his feet instead.

"Jesus!" I exclaim, covering my mouth with my hand.

Tom glances up at me worriedly and tries a weak smile. "No, just me," he says, then, stroking his beard, "though I understand the confusion."

I'm speechless. I shake my head. Upstairs I hear Jenny's door creak as she quietly closes it and realise that Tom has been there first.

Tom glances behind me and I step aside so he can enter. He drags his backpack over the threshold without looking me in the eye. My eyes are bulging and I can feel a muscle in the corner of my mouth twitching bizarrely.

"So?" I say, closing the door behind him.

Tom clears his throat. "Oh," he says. "So you're not gonna make this easy then."

I shrug and swallow hard. "Should I?" I say. "Do you think I should? Make it easy?"

Tom shakes his head and licks his lips.

"I thought you had it all worked out anyway," I say.

Tom frowns at me.

"Step three," I say.

Tom frowns and I realise he truly *doesn't* know what I'm talking about. "Step one, write a letter – well, a postcard. Step two, send flowers," I explain. "I kind of presumed you and Jenny had step three all worked out too."

Tom looks around the room. He looks like a cornered animal checking for escape routes. His eyes are watering. "That's not really fair," he says.

I close my eyes and shake my head. I can feel my cheeks burning. "Isn't it?" I say.

Tom steps forward to touch my arm but I jerk it away and shake my head incredulously at him. "Jesus Tom!" I say. "I mean, you don't actually think that you can just waltz in here..." But my voice fades out as I realise that this is, strangely, a replay of my scene with Hugo. That's exactly what I said to Hugo. Or is it just what I *wanted* to say to Hugo? What I should have said to Hugo. It's a peculiar moment of confusion. I wonder if I'm not getting my anger mixed up.

Tom's head is bowed, but he's looking up at me. His face is pale and the effect of his dark pupils, the whites of his eyes, actually makes him look quite dangerous. "I don't know what I *can* say," he says. "I don't know what to do to..."

"Of course you don't," I say bitterly. "Jenny's not here." I wince at the meanness of my words, but it's too late. It's said.

Tom's eyes are watering, and his voice cracks slightly as he says, "Jenny said you..."

I nod and blink slowly, my suspicions confirmed. "*What?*" I whistle. "What did she say?"

Tom shrugs and shakes his head.

I nod him on. "Go on Tom, I'm dying to know," I say.

Tom shakes his head and takes a step back towards the door. "She said you still have feelings for me," he says, looking me in the eye.

I turn away and look towards the window where Paloma is sitting on a cushion - asleep and unaware of the drama unfolding. I look at a book on the sideboard – anything to avoid looking at Tom.

He snorts sadly. "But you look more like you *hate* me," he says with difficulty.

I shake my head slowly and chew my lip.

"I don't know what to say Mark," Tom says. "I don't know what you want me to say."

I shake my head again. "You're pathetic Tom. You know that?"

Tom's half closes his eyes. It's as if I have slapped his face.

"I mean," I continue, tapping the side of my head. "Is anyone actually in there?"

Tom stares at his feet and moves his weight uncomfortably from foot to foot.

"What I want Tom… What I want*ed* was for you to actually get off your fucking arse and be… bothered," I say. "I wanted you to explain yourself, to apologise, and to make some fucking effort to make things right."

Tom frowns at me and swallows. "But I…" he says.

"None of this is from you," I say, waving my hand at the flowers, the card, the bag. "None of this is even your fucking *idea.*"

Tom shakes his head. His eyes are streaming and his face is swelling.

"It's just sad," I say.

Tom reaches for his bag. "I'm sorry," he says. "I thought…"

"Did you?" I say. "Did you *actually* think at all?"

Tom shakes his head and turns towards the door. "I should go," he says.

I open my mouth to say, "*Go!*" but I stop myself.

Tom peeps at me through the gap in the door as he pulls it closed behind him.

"And tell Jenny I don't like fucking roses," I say.

I rub my eyes and pace madly around the room. I slap the wall – it hurts my hand. I stomp to the bathroom and wash my face.

I sit on the sofa and think, *"How the fuck did we get here?"* How did the dream of reunion with Tom end up such a disaster? How did we get so… so *stuck*?

Of course it's Jenny's fault for intervening, for lying to me, for turning our lives into her very own scripted melodrama.

I suck my front teeth. My anger – suddenly focused against Jenny - crescendos. *"How dare she!"* I think.

I stand and swiping my keys from the sideboard I head upstairs. I couldn't give a fuck if Sarah's asleep. Jenny is gong to find out what's on my mind.

It's Tom who opens the door. Obvious of course, but it truly hadn't crossed my mind. *"He doesn't even have the balls to fuck off properly,"* I think.

Tom looks very pink. Everything about him has turned a deep hue of pink.

"I just wanted to say..." Tom starts to say, but I interrupt him.

"I didn't come to see you," I say turning away.

"She's out," Tom says behind me. "So you'll have to listen to me."

I snort derisively and glare back at him, suddenly hesitant to truly walk away. This feels like a last chance reprieve, and something about the spunk in his voice – *finally!* – makes me pause.

"Can you think of anything to say?" I say, meanly. "Without Jenny?"

Tom shakes his head. "That's horrible," Tom whispers. "You're just being horrible."

Devoid of a comeback, I shrug.

"You think you're so clever," Tom says. "So witty... But you're just fucking everything..."

I wave a hand in front of Tom's face. "Hey, Tom!" I say. "Hello? I'm *not* the one who fucked everything up."

Tom nods. "I know," he says, his tone carefully controlled. "*I* did."

I sigh furiously.

"But you *are* fucking it up now," he says. "I'm trying to..."

I shake my head. "There's nothing left *to* fuck up," I say.

Tom reaches out. His hand hovers an inch away from my arm. He looks into my eyes and leans forward. "I think there is," he says. "I *love* you."

I shake my head and sigh in despair.

"But I don't know..." Tom's voice wobbles. "I don't know what to do," he says.

My anger is subsiding and the taut, shiny feeling is being replaced with a swollen, marshmallow puffiness. My head feels huge and vague. I slide to crouching position and lean against the door-jamb.

"Tell me how to fix it," Tom says. "Tell me what I can do and I'll do it."

"But you did *nothing* Tom," I say. "I mean why does someone have to *tell* you what to do Tom? Why should *I* have to tell you?"

"Because I'm not a fucking mind reader," Tom says. "I didn't know what to do, I didn't know if there *was* anything I could do."

"And you know," I say, laughing sourly. "*Anything* would have done."

Tom touches my arm, and I let his hand remain. He crouches down so that he's in my line of sight and looks into my eyes again.

"I know how bad I let you down," he says. "I really do. That's why I didn't think there was a way, that's why I couldn't see how... But I called Jenny – just to find out how you were, and when she said..."

"*You* called *her*?" I say.

Tom blinks quizzically. "*Yeah*," he says. "and she told me what you said. That's the only reason I came." He moves his hand up to my shoulder. "I'll do anything babe," he says. "But you have to tell me what."

I shake my head in disbelief. "But why?" I say. "Why do I?"

Tom takes a deep breath and leans towards me. His forehead is almost touching mine. "Because you're the one who has to forgive," he says. "You're the only one who knows what it will take... What it will take for you to forgive me."

I rub my forehead and look around the landing, suddenly aware that we are having this most private of discussions in the most public of spaces.

"Come inside," Tom says.

I sit numbly on Jenny's sofa until he returns with hankies and glasses of water. Tom pulls up the pouf and we sit in silence staring at our feet. It's as if we're both embarrassed to go any further.

"I've really missed you," I mumble. Letting the words out is a major victory over my ego.

Tom nods. "It's been hellish," he says. "I've been so depressed."

"But you think I can tell you how..." I say shaking my head. "But even *I* don't know how to forgive you."

"I know," Tom says quietly.

"And it's not so much what happened. It's not so much you and Dante," I say.

Tom frowns at me.

"It's this…" I say, gesturing with the palm of my hand. "It's these *four* months. *Four months* Tom."

He nods again. "I know," he says.

"And the fact that I just don't understand why…"

"I know," Tom says quietly.

"I don't know how to trust you anymore," I say.

"I know, but maybe with time…" Tom says. I raise an eyebrow and he continues, "Maybe, if you gave me another chance, maybe then, you know, after a while you'd see…"

I sit back and pinch my nose, which has started to run.

"One day you might look back and see that I never *did* let you down again," Tom says. "I mean, I wouldn't you know," he says. "You know that at least, *right*?"

I shrug and drop my hand to my lap. "Do I?" I say.

Tom sighs and looks away. "No," he says. "Of course you don't."

He stands and turns his back to me and moves to the window. He suddenly looks like a beaten man – like someone who is in the throws of giving in to the inevitable end of this relationship.

All the failures of the past wash over me. A huge wave of fatigue envelops me. And it's suddenly not what I want. It's not what I want at all.

I force myself to stand and move to his side. I look out at the street below. "Maybe we could try," I say. It almost kills me to say it. "Maybe we could see what happens," I add.

Tom turns to face me and bites his lip. His Adam's apple bobs as he swallows; his eyes are tearing. "That would be good," he says. "I'd really like that."

It's funny really – well, *almost* funny. The things in life that you think you will never have, the things you spend years wanting and working towards and then suddenly forget about. And then there are the things you spend years wanting, and when you get them they're just not what you thought they were.

As the plane descends through the layer of cloud towards Gatwick airport, I can't help but wonder if I really want Tom at all.

It's strange to say, but it seems I've spent a lot of energy worrying about completely the wrong thing. I thought the issue would be whether I could learn to forgive Tom, whether I could learn to love Tom in the same old way. It turns out that the issue is whether I can continue to love a Tom who bears so little resemblance to the Tom I met, or at least the Tom I thought I met, that he might as well not be the same person at all.

The plane hits the tarmac with an unnerving bash, and I wonder, so to speak, which Tom is the real one. The bubbly, cheeky, do anything for a laugh Tom I used to date, or the sullen, untidy, big-spending hard working, guy I'm on my way to spend Christmas with.

I fight my way through the last minute travellers swarming around the airport, and onto the Brighton-bound train. It's full of office workers knocking off early, heading home with alcohol in their blood and gifts in their colourful paper bags. Momentarily my mood lifts. After all, who can resist Christmas?

But when I let myself into Tom's basement flat, my heart starts to sink. The curtains are still drawn and the place smells musty. There's even a vague twang of something sweet, something a little *too* sweet. That rotten-fruit-in-dustbin smell of decay.

I swipe open the curtains and fiddle with the catch and force open the big sash window. Cold air blasts in. I turn back to face the room expecting the worst. But it's even worse than last time.

My eyes scan the room, slowly cataloguing the desolation. On top of the TV sits a dinner plate caked with dried tomato sauce. In front of the TV stands a large unopened cardboard box. The writing says it's a flat screen LCD TV. In front of that sits a pair of shoes, dirty socks sprout from the tops. The glass coffee table – hard to keep clean at the best of times – looks like another used dinner plate.

I shake my head and move towards the sofa. A dirty work-shirt is draped over one armrest, a still-knotted tie lies on one of the seat-cushions. Another dried up dinner plate is in the process of sliding down the side between the armrest and the seat.

Every surface is covered in a thick layer of dust. I go to run my finger along the mantelpiece, and notice a squiggling line cutting through the dust indicating that Tom has already done so.

He's never liked housework – that I know – but this is getting out of hand.

I shuck my aviator jacket and swipe the dirty clothes from around the room and head through to the kitchen.

Tom's laundry basket is overflowing, so I turn to the washing machine hoping to use it as secondary storage, but it too is full, not only with clothes but with water too. I ball up the clothes and throw them into the corner and, with a disgusted shake of my head, I return to the lounge for a dirty-plate collection.

The kitchen sink is stacked high with dirty dishes, so I lift a pile clear and dump them on a cardboard pizza carton on the table. Half a pizza is still in the box. "For fuck's sake Tom!" I say to no one in particular.

I roll my sleeves thinking that this isn't how I had imagined spending Christmas Eve. "*Still,*" I figure. "*Season of goodwill and all that...*"

I take a deep breath and – imagining Tom's face when he sees the soon-to-be-realised transformation – I do a 360 degree scan of the room and set to work.

By 7 PM when I hear his key in the lock, the place is looking almost normal. I lean out of the kitchen so that I can see his reaction.

"Hello!" he says, smiling and rolling his eyes. "Sorry I'm so late but I've had a bitch of a day."

He's wearing one of his new suits – a silky grey one, and a deep blue shirt with a spread collar. He looks fabulously sharp; it's a bizarre contrast with his living space.

He pulls off his jacket and throws it onto the sofa and then notices the changes. "God you *cleaned!*" he says, walking towards me. "You didn't have to do that," he adds softly.

I pull a face. "Well, really, I kind of did," I tell him. "It was pretty disgusting."

Tom frowns at me as if I'm telling fibs. "It was a bit messy I guess," he says. "I've been so busy… Anyway, cheers."

I'd expected more, but I instruct myself to remain calm. No point getting upset about housework on Christmas Eve. "I couldn't get the washing machine to work," I say.

Tom wrinkles his nose and nods. "I know," he says. "It's broken." He steps forward and holding my biceps, he pecks me on the lips. "Hello!" he says.

I slide a hand down to his arse and we kiss. The feel of his buttocks through the silky fabric gives me the beginnings of an erection, but Tom pulls away.

"Let me change," he says, pushing towards the bedroom, "and we can go eat."

I frown. "Out?" I say. "I was thinking…"

"Yeah," Tom interrupts. "I booked a table at that new Japanese place," he says. "I've been wanting to go there for ages."

I sigh. I had been thinking more of a cosy night in around the fire with a bottle of wine. "I thought we could stay in – I've been travelling all day," I say. "And cleaning."

Tom appears in the doorway to the bedroom, one leg in a pair of crumpled jeans. "There's no food in anyway," he says. "And that place is supposed to be the bees knees."

He pulls what looks like a brand new *Surfin' Life* sweatshirt over his head. It's fluorescent orange with a huge *Surfin' Life* logo across the front. As he hops across the kitchen towards me, he pulls on a pair of trainers.

"Okay?" he says, pointing his palms at me. I'm apparently supposed to approve his outfit. I push my lips out. He looks like some adolescent Californian.

"I liked the suit better," I say plaintively. "And what's with the big logo? I thought you hated logos."

Tom shrugs. "You're just a suit slut," he says, adding, "Anyway, I like the logo… It's kind of cool… Don't you think?"

I shrug and nod my head. "I guess," I say. Remembering suddenly how much I dislike Japanese food, I add, "Hey Tom, isn't that Japanese place like, really expensive? Because I'm not really that…"

Tom has pulled on a coat and is heading for the door. He pauses and looks back at me. "Don't worry about it," he says. "It's reserved. And we're late. Call it your Christmas present."

I open my mouth to make a final attempt at nudging the evening in a different direction, but Tom – unlike his washing machine – is on spin cycle. There's no stopping him now.

"Come on!" he says, opening the front door. "We'll be late."

I sigh and grab my jacket. As I walk past him he pats my behind. "Hey, you get to go in the new car too," he says. "I forgot you haven't seen it yet."

I close my eyes and take a deep breath. When I open them again I'm out in the street and I'm grinning.

"Wow, yeah!" I say with forced enthusiasm. "Which one is it?"

I wiggle Sarah up and down upon my knee.

"This one's very calm," I say.

Jenny nods. "Yeah, maybe she missed you," she says. "It's been kind of calm around here."

"Did you have a nice Christmas though?" I ask.

Jenny shrugs. "I guess so," she says. "The weather was amazing, so we went for lots of walks. I'm still trying to walk off all the weight I put on. Oh, I changed my French teacher. That's been fun."

"Fun?"

Jenny raises an eyebrow. "Well, I just lied to the old one and told her I was moving back to England. But the new one's really nice. We've been meeting up and having coffee and stuff. It's much more conversational French."

"I thought you were doing okay really," I say. "Every time I hear you speak you seem to be getting by just fine."

Jenny nods. "Yeah, it was just all a bit formal. And dull. And slow. If I want to think about staying then I need to get better. And fast," she says. "So I can think about finding a job and investigate childcare and everything."

"Well, I hope you do," I say. "I kind of like having you around."

"So you're not moving to Brighton?" Jenny asks. "I was kind of thinking that if you had a good time with Tom... over Christmas..."

"Tom is so weird at the moment," I tell her. "That's hardly likely. Plus it rained every day. You forget just how bad the British weather can be."

Jenny nods and sips her tea. "So how *is* darling Tom?" she asks.

I sigh and wonder how much to tell her.

"You say he's *weird*?" Jenny asks.

I shake my head as I search for words. "It's really strange," I say. "It's kind of like he's someone completely different at the moment. I think I'm waiting to see if he stays this way or if the old Tom is coming back," I tell her.

Jenny frowns and plumps a pillow as she settles in. "Tell me all about it," she says.

I lean over to check Sarah's face – she's being remarkably quiet. It turns out she has closed her eyes. She's working her tiny mouth as if she's chewing gum.

"His new job seems to take like 110% of him," I tell her. "I suppose that's the first difference. He's working twelve or fourteen hours a day."

Jenny nods. "I never really understood what he does," she comments.

I shake my head. "Well, that's one of Tom's weirdeties too. Does that exist, *weirdeties*?"

Jenny shrugs in a way that means, *whatever, continue.*

"Well, he won't talk about it."

"It's foreign exchange right?"

I nod. "Yeah. That's about all we know. He wears sharp suits, works long days, it's something to do with foreign exchange."

"And he works for his uncle."

I nod in agreement. "He works for his uncle and earns loads-a-dosh. But other than that... I mean, if you ask him, he just says, "Oh *perlease*.." As if he just can't bear to talk about it."

Jenny nods. "I can understand that," she says. "It's not so strange. I was like that when I was in advertising."

I nod. "Sure," I say. "But he's just not himself somehow. He's spending loads... He has a new car, a new TV, new clothes. But on the other hand his place looks like a bloody squat. Well, it did until I got there and cleaned it all up. The fridge is empty and the washing machine, kettle and Hoover are all broken."

"So why doesn't he just replace them?" Jenny asks. "I mean, if he's loaded."

I shrug. "That's what I mean. He's just... well, *strange* really. He was managing without a washing machine by just wearing new clothes all the time."

Jenny frowns. "That is a *bit* peculiar I suppose." She shrugs. "But..."

I raise an eyebrow.

"He's forty soon isn't he?"

I nod. "Yeah, in June."

Jenny shrugs. "Maybe that's something to do with it."

I laugh. "What, you mean he's having some kind of midlife crisis?"

Jenny frowns thoughtfully. "Who knows," she says. "But was Christmas fun despite it all?" she asks. "I mean; you two are okay, right?"

I laugh. "It was just bizarre," I tell her. "It was like staying with a stranger. A suit-wearing, big-spending, restaurant-going, slovenly... fairly sexy stranger."

Jenny grins. "Sounds quite fun really," she says.

"He's putting on loads of weight," I say. "So far it suits him, but you know what he used to be like about going to the gym."

Jenny shakes her head vaguely. "He doesn't go at all anymore?"

I shake my head. "Nope," I say. "He just buys new clothes when they don't fit. Or when they get dirty. Still, I got the washing machine replaced. He bought this amazing Daewoo thing that washes and dries so nothing needs ironing. It cost a fortune, though I'm not convinced he'll use it."

Jenny leans across to take Sarah from me and I realise that she is asleep. I lean forward and hand over the warm package.

"You're not jealous of him are you?" Jenny asks.

I frown. "I don't think so," I say. "Why?"

She shrugs. "It just sounds like you might be feeling worried he's leaving you behind."

I cock my head to one side to show that I'm fully considering this theory. But then I shake my head. "Nah," I say. "That's not it. Really. I'm more *concerned* about him really. He doesn't seem to be looking after himself."

Jenny frowns. "I thought he was spending..."

"Yeah, but not on his basic needs, you know?" I sigh. "It's hard to explain. But he just doesn't seem to be himself."

"I think you're making a fuss about nothing," Jenny tells me. "It sounds like he's just enjoying his new found wealth."

I shake my head. "No," I say. "There's something else... something wrong."

Jenny frowns at me.

"What?" I ask.

"You're not thinking of leaving him are you?" she says. "Not after all that..."

I shake my head and interrupt her. "Nah," I say. "Not for now anyway. It's funny really. But I kind of want to see what happens. If that makes any sense."

"See what happens?" Jenny repeats.

I nod. "Yeah... I'm waiting to find out if this is the real Tom or some sort of blip. I'm waiting to see if he'll get dirtier, or sloppier or whatever – if he *can* get any sloppier, or if he'll pull himself together. I'm still trying to understand who he is I suppose."

Jenny nods thoughtfully. "Well, you want to," she says. "You want to make the effort to do that. I supposed that's what counts... more than anything."

I nod. "Maybe." I say. "Maybe I'm just at a point in my life where... I feel like I've always run away, sort of, closed the book before the end. Walked out of the film, you know, when it got to the gory bit, or the boring bit... or the sad bit... But I think I'm bored with that... Bored with prologues. I feel like I want to read the whole story this time. I want to know how it ends."

Jenny grins broadly. "Sounds like love to me," she says.

I snort. "Maybe... though..." I shake my head.

"Though what?" Jenny asks.

"Oh, nothing," I say. "We'll see."

Tom sits on the sofa opposite and yawns and scratches his balls. He's wearing boxer shorts – only boxer shorts – and his hair is flattened on one side and jutting out madly on the other. I drape my suit bag over the back of a chair and pull up a pouf.

"I'm sorry it's a mess again," Tom says unconvincingly.

A *mess* doesn't really describe it. The room looks as if some giant has picked it up and shaken it around like a snow-globe. Nothing, and I mean *nothing* is in the right place. Just on the sofa, where Tom is sitting, I catalogue: a pile of washing, a Marks & Spencer bag, a shoe, a toilet roll, and, perhaps most bizarrely as Tom has no garden, a pair of shears.

"I just haven't had time," Tom continues. "What with the arrangements and everything."

I shrug. I'm getting used to Tom's new, messy persona. I'm more concerned about Tom himself. "I thought your uncle was dealing with all that," I say.

Tom shrugs. "There's still a million phone calls to make," Tom says. "Anyway, Claude and dad never got on. I'm the only one who knows who to call and stuff."

I nod thoughtfully, and move my head from side to side trying to look Tom in the eye, trying to detect some sign of sadness, some sign of suffering. It's not that I *want* him to be sad particularly. It's just that I can't believe he isn't. "What about you?" I say. "Were you two... *close*? I mean, you never talked about him much."

Tom yawns again and pushes out a lip. "Yeah," he says, matter-of-factly. "Not as close as to mum maybe, but, well, *quite* close I suppose."

He rubs a hand across his belly. He's put on enough weight that it's starting to bulge over the waistband.

"Are you okay Tom?" I ask. "I mean... You *seem* okay."

Tom shrugs and nods. "Yeah," he says. "I seem to be fine."

I nod. "You seem almost a little bit *too* fine," I say.

Tom shrugs. "I guess I was shocked on Wednesday. I mean no one expects... no one expects that to happen. But I think I'm sort of over it now."

I frown and bite my bottom lip. "I doubt that really," I say quietly. "But, well, if you're okay for now... Well, you're okay for now, aren't you."

Tom stands and smiles tightly. "Yeah, whatever," he says dismissively. "You want some tea? Or coffee?"

I swivel as I watch him cross the room. "What time do we have to leave?" I ask.

Tom pauses at the doorway to the kitchen and checks his watch. "Oh, about eleven will do," he says. "It takes about three hours to get there, so… Yeah – eleven… *ish*."

I ask Tom for an iron but he just throws one of his stock of new shirts at me. I rip open the packaging and, side-by-side we slip on our identical, brand-new shirts. They are crisp and white, rigid with newness.

We help with each other's cufflinks and pull on our black suit trousers, and then we stand side by side and knot our black ties. Our uniform of sorrow. We look like something from *Men in Black*. Actually I think we look *hot*.

I straighten my knot and turn to face Tom. "So?" I say.

He nods noncommittally. "You'll do," he says. "Though *this*…" And here he grabs at my dick through the fabric of my trousers. "Is *entirely* inappropriate."

I pull a face. "I know," I say. "It's just seeing you… In your posh gear and everything. It'll go away."

Tom caresses my dick slightly with his thumb and then steps forward and pecks me on the lips. "It'll have to, I'm afraid," he says, turning and pulling his jacket from a hanger. "Cos we need to get moving I think."

I slide back a cuff and check my watch. "Eleven," I say. "Just gone."

Tom nods. "Yep, let's hit the road."

The drive to Wolverhampton takes exactly three hours. Tom remains glassy and hermetic. He is driving more slowly than usual and the green countryside glides past the tinted windows of his new Mercedes silently, effortlessly.

It's a strange space here inside this luxury car; the unexpected silence, the smell not of the countryside but of leather, of polish… The suspension is making a near perfect job of ironing out the bumps, the air conditioning maintains a perfectly controlled 21.5 degrees. I can't help but think back to what Dante said about quality and luxury – for clearly, there is plenty of luxury here. And yet he's right... There is no life here, none at all. It's all numb and smooth; all dead and senseless. I would rather be on a motorbike being hot and cold and rattled to bits.

I glance at Tom from time to time and decide that he looks like a robot – a sort of *Max Headroom* virtual-reality executive. He certainly doesn't look like a man – my man – going to his father's funeral. I guess he's bottling up, and I decide that that's probably normal. I wonder when the cork will blow.

But it doesn't happen. Not during the tiny service in the disinfectant-scented crematorium, not during the moribund gathering at the next-door neighbour's house, and not during the drive home.

Tom is quieter than usual, but that is the only sign that this is anything other than a normal day.

"Your uncle seems nice," I say.

Tom snorts and checks his wing mirror before replying, "He isn't."

I didn't really think he *was*. It was merely a dishonest attempt at communication. "Who were the guys with him?" I ask. "The stocky ones."

"Work colleagues," Tom says.

I nod to myself and sigh silently. "They look like gangsters," I say. "Or bodyguards."

Tom snorts lightly again. "They are," he says.

I wonder if he means gangsters or bodyguards. "I tried to talk to one of them. I asked him who he was... he just walked away," I say. I look at Tom and wait for him to reply, but after a moment realise that he isn't going to, so I turn and look out the window. "Just making conversation," I mutter neutrally.

Tom coughs. "Yeah," he says kindly. "I know."

"I guess you just want to be quiet with your thoughts," I say.

"Yeah," Tom says. "That's best."

I watch as some new-build town spins past behind the window, the sun setting behind the rows of identical redbrick houses.

"Actually there *is* something you could do," Tom says.

"Yeah?" I say turning to look back at him.

He fidgets in his seat awkwardly. "Yeah, if you really want to ease my pain, well..."

I frown at him. "Yeah?" I say.

Tom wrinkles his brow. "Nah," he says. "Doesn't matter."

He runs a hand down his front, across his tie and rests it on his lap.

"What Tom?" I say. "Tell me."

He coughs again and grins. "I was just thinking... well. I thought maybe..."

I shift in my seat to face him fully. He has my attention now. "*What?*" I say with a little laugh.

"Well," Tom says. "A blow-job wouldn't go amiss."

I blink at him slowly and smile lopsidedly. "A *blow job?*" I repeat.

Tom flicks his eyes at me, and lifts his tie and flaps it a little to the right. A rounded hillock pokes from his lap. "It would really help," he says.

"You want a blow-job!" I say, bemused. "Here... Now?"

Tom shrugs.

"And is that... What was the word you used?"

Tom grins. "Appropriate?" he says.

I nod and slide a hand to his lap. "Yeah, that's it. Would that be *appropriate?*"

Tom coughs again and fidgets, settling further into his seat. "Oh," he says. "A blow-job would be *entirely* appropriate."

I laugh and peck him on the cheek and unzip his fly, revealing the white of his shirttails.

"*Would* it?" I say, laughing dryly. I glance nervously up at the window and say, "Okay, just don't overtake any lorries." And then, as I lean towards his lap, as he places a hand behind my head and pushes it down, his dick pokes through the opening, sprouting out like a seedling, pushing out and up until it reaches the tip of his tie.

"Ummm," Tom says, resting a hand on the back of my head. "Like that."

It's hot tonight – stuffy. As I fidget my foot discovers a cool corner of the bedclothes. I move instinctively towards it, gradually working my way over until I am entirely on the other side of the bed. I'm on the point of drifting back to sleep when I realise that this is Tom's side of the bed.

I groan and roll onto my back, then lean over and fumblingly reach for the alarm clock. It takes a while before my eyes will focus enough to read the figures – 4:32 AM.

I cough to clear my throat, and then drag my body – still heavy with sleep – into sitting position. I groan tiredly and stand.

In the lounge, Tom – who remains unaware of my presence – has his back turned to me; he's occupied wiping the sideboard. Between us, a four-foot-high pile of random objects blocks the middle of the room.

So as not to scare him, I clear my throat but Tom jumps anyway.

"Oh, hello," he says in a bubbly voice. "What are you doing up?"

I click my tongue against the roof of my mouth and mutter, "Thirsty... What are *you* doing up?" I approach the junk pile and pick up a videocassette – *Ariston Video Presents – Leathermen II*.

"I couldn't sleep," Tom says with a shrug. "And I was bored... And the place needs cleaning..."

I put *Leathermen II* back on the pile, balancing it on top of a wobbly inkjet printer. "And what's all this?" I ask. "It looks like you're building a bonfire."

Tom smiles. "Nah..." he says. "It would be good though... to just burn it all. But no, I'm just putting everything that's in the wrong place, kind of, well... in *one* place. Stage two is I put everything back where it should be."

I nod. "Very organised," I say, walking around the pile and touching his arm. "But it's 4 AM; why don't you come back to bed?"

Tom shrugs and my hand falls away. "I can't sleep," he says. "There's no point just lying there. It just winds me up."

"Come back to bed and we can *not-sleep* together," I say, touching Tom's arm again.

This time he jerks his arm away from me. "I'm fine," he says, tetchily. "Just..." He swallows, and when he continues his voice is forcibly calmer. "Go back to bed," he says.

I shrug. "Okay," I say. "You know where I am."

I sit bolt upright; I am not sure why I am awake – a noise, a crash, a bad dream? The cold light of dawn is filtering into the room.

"Tom?" I call. I yawn and slide my legs to the edge of the bed. "*Tom?*" I repeat.

I hear a noise from the lounge – a voice, a groan maybe. As I scratch my head and stand, I hear it again. "*Tom?*" I repeat, stumblingly heading for the lounge.

The flat is quiet and empty; well, empty that is, except for the pile of stuff, which has grown a little since I went back to bed.

Beyond the mound lies a stepladder. I frown and step forward. It is only then that I see Tom, lying in the strangest of positions.

He's cradled, as it were, by the oval, steel frame of the coffee table. His arms and shoulders hang outside the loop, as do his legs.

As I frown and mumble, "*Tom?*" his head lolls towards me, and only then do I grasp what has happened; only then do I see the shards of glass lying beneath him.

"Shit Tom," I say, instantly awake. "Are you okay?"

Tom looks at me woozily. "I think I hit my head," he says.

He tries to lift himself from the table but as he straightens, he winces and gasps. "And, I've cut my..." he says, stretching and twisting in an attempt at looking beneath him. "Shit!"

I carefully step over him, straddling his legs and grasp his hands. "Careful where you put your feet," I say. "There's glass everywhere."

Tom nods. "Yeah," he says. "I can feel it."

"Okay, and... *Up!*" I grunt as I pull him forwards.

Tom blinks and sways a little on his feet, and then frowns and peers down at his side. "Shit," he says. "Look at that."

A three-inch shard of glass is jutting from the flesh just above his hip. It's shaped like a curved dagger. I lift another chunk of glass carefully out of the way and reposition my feet so that I can inspect the wound.

"Ouch," I say with feeling. "Looks like I'm taking you to A&E."

Tom rolls his eyes. "*Really?*" he says plaintively. "Do you think?"

"Yeah," I say. "Look, be careful. Don't cut your feet as well." I step carefully over the broken remains of the coffee table and head through to the bedroom where I quickly dress.

When I return, Tom is standing in front of the angle-poise lamp grasping the shard of glass.

"Tom!" I say. "Wait, let them do it at the ho..." but as I say it he gasps and pulls the chunk of glass from his side.

"Phew!" he says wincingly examining his wound. "It wasn't so deep after all."

"Wow!" I exclaim, crouching beside him. "What a man! Maybe take you to the hospital anyway though," I say. "There might still be glass or something stuck inside."

Tom lays the bloody glass dagger down on the sideboard and then frowns and inspects his palm and tuts.

"What a *twat*!" he says, pointing his hand at me. A thick line of blood is oozing from a deep gash across the palm.

"Shit Tom!" I say. "Have you just done that?"

Tom nods sheepishly. "Yeah," he says. "*Sorry.*"

The Accident and Emergency waiting room is entirely empty. A black nurse with a Jamaican accent and a sleepy smile asks Tom a few questions – blood group, vaccine status, previous conditions, current drug regime, and then leads him through to a cubicle down the hall.

When she returns, she slouches at her desk, chews a biro and smiles at me.

"So how *exactly* did he do that?" she asks me. Her voice is full of laughter so I smile back and shrug.

"Cleaning windows," I say. "He fell off the stepladder."

"He fell though da window?!" the nurse exclaims.

I grin at her. "Nah," I tell her, "... onto the coffee table."

"And what prey, was he doin' cleanin' da windows at..." she looks at her watch, "Six in the mornin' Was they *that* dirty?"

Her Jamaican accent is luscious. It makes me grin even more. I shrug. "Your guess is as good as mine."

She nods knowingly. "That'll be the Prozac," she says. "It happen' all the time you know."

I nod thoughtfully. "Yeah," I say. "He didn't tell me about that." I shake my head. "I didn't know he was on Prozac."

The nurse nods. "Everyone' on Prozac," she says. "That's the trouble of it."

I sigh. "His dad just died," I say with a shrug. "Maybe that's why."

She nods. "Yeah," she says softly. "But in the end, I is one of them people who thinks drugs is not the answer to everything, you know?"

I nod. "I know," I say. "Me too."

Tom sits and stares at his bandaged hand. He looks confused, uncomprehending as to quite how or indeed *when* this thing happened to him. I take a seat beside him and sigh. The air whistles through my nose.

"You okay?" I ask. "You look a bit dazed really."

Tom nods slowly, silently staring at his hand. He shakes his head and continues to inspect the bandage.

"You must be tired," I say. "Don't you want to go back to bed?"

Tom pouts and shakes his head. He licks his lips, opens his mouth to speak, and then pauses for a moment.

For some reason I am expecting that he will say something important, something profound even. But what he eventually says is merely, "How was the Merc'? Did you enjoy driving it?"

I cough. "Yeah," I say vaguely. "It's nice. Um, smooth... and powerful."

Tom nods. "You don't really give a damn about the car," he says, adding with a shrug, "Neither do I, when it comes down to it."

I shrug benevolently. "It's nice," I say. "It's a very good car. And very useful for going to hospitals."

Tom snorts and lays his hand, palm-up, across his knees.

"Are you okay, Tom?" I ask. "I mean, obviously you're sad, but, well, I'm worried about you. Generally I mean. Even before all this..."

Tom nods and stands. "Yeah, well," he says. "Don't be."

I nod thoughtfully.

"You want tea?" he asks, turning towards the kitchen.

"Yeah," I say. "You sure you don't want me to do..." But Tom is already there. I can hear him filling the kettle.

I sigh wearily and move across the room to the smashed coffee table. I prop the stepladder against the wall, and start to collect the smaller chunks of glass. "You'll need a new coffee table," I shout, but, over the noise of the kettle, Tom doesn't seem to hear me.

I wrap most of the glass – all except the biggest chunks – in an old copy of *The Argus,* and then, aware that Tom has been gone a long time, I follow him through to the kitchen.

Two mugs sit ready, each containing a tea bag; the kettle steams gently.

Tom is sitting on the tiled floor, back to the fridge. Silent tears are streaming down his cheeks.

I pause for a moment, taking this in, then blink slowly and slide to his side, laying an arm across his shoulders. "That's good," I say. "You have to let go sometime... you can't just keep it all inside."

Tom flicks his watery eyes towards me and returns his gaze to his lap. A drip is hanging from the end of his nose, so I stand and grab a length of kitchen roll, then slide back to the floor.

"I'm so sorry babe," I say, handing him the tissue. "I know how hard it is; really I do. I remember from when my own..."

Tom judders beside me in a sudden spasm of grief, gasps, and then continues to weep quietly.

I pull him against me and lean my head against his, as though this might somehow lessen the pain he is feeling, as if I can share it between the two of us. I would happily take on half, were that possible. My own eyes water.

After a couple of minutes Tom's sobs wane. "I don't..." he attempts. But then he pauses and blows his nose.

"Yeah?" I ask, wiping a tear from his cheek with my thumb.

Tom shrugs and gently lifts my arm away in order to stand. "Finish the tea?" he asks, heading back to the lounge.

Tom nurses the mug as if it were winter; he looks hunched and cold. "I don't think the Prozac is working," he says with a sad, ironic snort.

I put my mug down on the floor and take his un-bandaged hand in mine. "It takes a while," I say. "I think it takes a couple of weeks before it kicks in."

Tom nods.

"And it won't, you know, make the grief go away. You just have to... well... You just have to go *through* grief... Like a tunnel... Eventually you come out the other side."

Tom nods. "I thought it was working before though," he says. "I felt a bit better in January."

I nod and swallow as I think about this. "January," I repeat. "So how long have you been on it?" I ask. "I mean, I didn't know... You never said."

Tom shrugs. "October," he says. "I started in October."

I nod and sigh. I think, "*So that's why he's been so weird.*"

"I just feel like..." he says. He shrugs. "I feel like there's no point, you know?"

I furrow my brow. "It will pass though," I say, "...that feeling. I know it feels like you'll never get over it. But it *does* fade, in the end. You have to trust. And wait." I shrug. "There's not a lot else you can do."

Tom clears his throat to speak. A pedestrian pauses outside his window. The shadow causes us both to look up. We can only see the bottom of his suit trousers where they meet shiny black shoes.

When he moves on, Tom clears his throat again. "It's not Dad," he says, his voice a whisper. "He's better out of it..."

I frown in incomprehension.

"It's all the rest," Tom says. "It's all the other shit."

I stroke his index finger between my own finger and thumb. "*What* rest babe?" I say. "What other shit?"

Tom shrugs. "Oh I don't know," he says.

I stroke his hand and wait for him to continue.

"I thought that if we got back together," he says, after a pause.

I bite my bottom lip. "Yeah?" I murmur weakly.

"I thought I'd be happy. Happier. I thought, you know, that that was *why* I was unhappy," he says. "Because we had split up."

I cough and release his finger, alarmed that we are suddenly discussing the shortcomings of our relationship. "Aren't you happy?" I say. "I mean, I didn't know... Aren't you happy with me?"

Tom frowns and shakes his head silently for a moment. "I don't know," he says. "I'm not happy. But, it's not specific... it's, well it's everything really."

I nod.

"I don't *think* it's us," Tom says. "It's the rest." His voice wavers. "Sometimes I just feel like..." He shrugs and shakes his head.

I stroke his back. "What?"

He shakes his head again and sighs. "I feel like I don't see the point anymore, you know?"

"In us?"

"In anything. I feel like, if I could, you know, just opt out, of the rest of my life... But I'm too much of a coward, you know, to..."

"That's not being a coward," I say. "Staying and fighting is brave. Opting out is the cowardly way."

"But what if, you know…" he says, his voice cracking. "What if you know that it's all…"

I frown at him.

"What if you know it's all *pointless*. That it isn't *going* to get any better," Tom says, a fresh tear sliding down his cheek. "I mean, if it's all shit, why do you *have* to carry on? Why can't you just…"

I run a hand across my head. "Tom, what's wrong? I mean… I understand that you're down, but, I don't know, give me some specifics here."

Tom shrugs. "It's like I said. It's everything."

I nod. "Like?"

"You wouldn't understand," Tom says quietly. "I'm not being funny, but, well, it's me…"

I shrug. "Try me," I say. "List them. List all the things that are wrong."

Tom stares at the ceiling for a moment. The light suddenly fades and we both look up to see the same pedestrian as before standing in front of the window.

"It's this dingy fucking flat," Tom says, standing.

"Where are you going?" I ask.

"To tell him to stand someplace else…"

"But Tom you can't just…"

But it seems that he can. I shake my head and sigh deeply as I see Tom's shadow mount the staircase beyond the window, see his bare feet and jeans join the poor man who just chose to stand in the wrong place.

When Tom returns he slumps back onto the sofa next to me and picks up his cup of tea.

"Jesus, what did you tell him?" I ask.

Tom shrugs. "I just asked him to stand somewhere else. I said he was blocking the light."

I shake my head. "That's…"

"Well he was," Tom says. "And it does my head in."

I frown. "Maybe you need to move," I say. "I mean, if it's the flat that's depressing you."

Tom shakes his head dolefully. "It's not just the flat, it's the world," he says.

"The world," I repeat.

"Yeah, George Bush," Tom says.

I frown. "George *Bush*," I repeat flatly.

"Yeah, and Iran, and Iraq, and the tsunami, and Live Eight..."

I nod.

"... and Blair," Tom says. "And nuclear power..."

I nod slowly. "I know what you *mean*," I say with a sigh. "But that's all... Well, it's all elsewhere, isn't it? Look out your window and everything's fine," I say.

Tom shakes his head. "But it isn't," he says. "Everything's fucked."

I shake my head. "But not *here*..." I say. "A hundred years ago you wouldn't even have known what was happening in Iraq."

"My life here is as fucked as anything else," Tom interrupts. "It's all... plastic bags and frozen food, bottled water and chemicals... and the shit vegetables we get here. Do you *remember* what the food tasted like in Italy?" he spits. "You can't even buy a fucking red pepper here that doesn't come in a plastic sealed package."

I nod. "Yeah, that's true, but..."

"And the car? You know? I mean, I wanted it, and truly, like, *minutes* after I picked it up..." he shrugs. "I just couldn't see the point. So I went out and bought a new TV..." He nods at the huge LCD screen. "But it's just full of Iraq and Iran, and Bush... Only *bigger*."

I nod. "Oh babe," I say. "It sounds like maybe you *are* depressed."

Tom shrugs. "That's what I said – the Prozac isn't working."

I nod. "Maybe," I say. "Maybe it isn't."

"But even if it did work," he says. "All of that stuff would be... I mean, it would still be true, yeah?"

I nod. "But there's other stuff," I say. "I mean, maybe the fact that you're depressed is making you focus on the wrong things."

Tom snorts. "So what *should* I focus on?" he asks. "Tell me!"

I shrug. "*I* don't know Tom," I say desperately. "Maybe you should think about what *you* want. What kind of life *you want*. And how to get it."

Tom drags his fingertips down across his cheeks distorting his features. "It's too late," he says, shaking his head.

I sigh and shake my head. "You're only forty, Tom," I say. "It's not too late for any…"

Tom shakes his head and interrupts me. "That's not what I mean," he says. "I mean, it's too late… It's the wrong era for what I want. The wrong époque."

I frown at him, so he expounds. "I should have been born a hundred years ago," he says. "When things were simpler. I was born in the wrong time."

"You would have been sent to war," I point out. "Or imprisoned… for buggery."

Tom nods. "I guess," he says. "So I wouldn't have fitted in then either… is what you're saying."

He shakes his head, sighs and stands. My hand falls away from his back.

"Sorry about all this," he says flatly. "I don't mean to dump on you… I… I think I'm going to go and lie down for a bit. I feel wiped out."

I blink slowly. "Go for it," I say. "I'll join you in a bit."

As I pick up the remaining shards of glass I think about Tom, about George Bush and vacuum packed vegetables; about nuclear power and Mercedes cars; frozen dinners and bottled water, and I wonder that we're not all taking Prozac. But of course, as the black nurse said, nearly everyone *is* taking Prozac these days.

The waiting pedestrian walks past the window again, and the light in the flat momentarily dims. I'm glad Tom isn't here to see it.

I feel totally overcome, flooded by his sadness. And it strikes me that Tom might be feeling suicidal, but it is *he* in fact who is being lucid. The madmen are the rest of us who manage to float through all of this with our stupid smiles on our stupid faces.

I open my eyes. The vision from my right eye is blocked by the plump pillow my head is resting on. Through the other I can see Tom. He's staring at the ceiling, apparently unaware that I am watching him.

I stretch and say, "God, I slept like a log, what time is it?"

Tom tips his head smoothly towards me. "You were snoring," he says, his voice monotone.

I roll onto my back. "Sorry," I say.

Tom shrugs. "It's okay," he says.

We lie like this for a moment, and then he says, a little unexpectedly, "Do you ever wish you were religious?"

The question stumps me for a moment. I roll onto my side and rest a hand on Tom's chest. "Not really," I say. "Why? Do you?" I figure that he's thinking about his dead father, about the possibility of an afterlife.

"Sometimes, yeah," he says. "Just to have someone to tell me what to do really. A priest. Or something."

I nod thoughtfully and then snort. "He'd probably tell you to get married and make babies," I say. "They have a tendency to homophobia. And paedophilia."

Tom half rolls his head towards me and says flatly, "Yeah, I guess so."

I run a finger along his shoulder.

"But we don't have any spiritual guidance anymore, do we?" he says. "There's no one to turn to for, you know... absolute answers."

I nod. "Maybe that's because we're wiser," I say. "Maybe we're clever enough to know that there aren't any. Absolute answers, that is."

"I used to ask my dad. When I was a kid, he always seemed to know what to do. It was nice."

I nod and sigh in empathy. "Yeah," I say. "And he's not around anymore."

Tom snorts. "Oh, he stopped having the answers years ago anyway," he says. "Once I got to thirty, well, anything I couldn't work out for myself, he didn't know either... I guess we catch them up."

"It's part of being a grown-up," I say quietly. "That realisation that you're on your own, that no one knows any better."

Tom nods. "I know," he says. "The trouble is, I don't know either. A guru would be good. Someone to say, do this, do that... I mean, I can see why all those people joined communes in the seventies, you know?"

I shuffle across the bed so that my side touches Tom's. He feels hot and sweaty. "You don't need a guru Tom," I tell him. "Or a commune. You just need to... to, re-set the sails. To work out a new destination."

Tom nods.

"It's normal I think," I say. "It's a forty thing, and a losing your parents thing. Life's not linear. You have to tack, to move a bit to the right, and a bit to the left, and try and find a direction that fits."

"You think this is *normal?*" Tom asks, his voice incredulous.

I sigh. "I think there are times when you have to question the direction you've taken. Sometimes you need to choose a new one. Sometimes you even have to turn around and go back."

"I guess," Tom says.

"And I think forty is one of those times. Well, for lots of people it is anyway."

Tom nods and lies silently for a minute. Then he says, very quietly, "I don't like my life though. I'm not sure I like myself much."

I sigh and stroke his shoulder again.

"I've been, I am, *so* unhappy..." His voice is taught and ready to crack anew.

I nod and sigh deeply. "Then you have to change it," I say.

Tom shakes his head. "I don't think I can," he says. "I don't think I know where to start."

I lie watching him for a moment. It strikes me, that – practically speaking, absolute-truth aside – Tom needs a lifeline. He needs some hope.

"You could..." I say. "Change things, I mean. I'd help you."

Tom smiles at me weakly. "You want to be my guru?"

I laugh. "You wanna be *mine*?" I say.

He shakes his head. "Nah," he says sadly.

"What *do* you want Tom?" I say. "What kind of life?"

Tom squints at the ceiling for a moment before replying. "I think I want to slow it all down," he says.

I remember him saying exactly that at Dante's farm. I frown and wait for him to continue.

"It's all too fast," he says. "Too shallow. Too disconnected."

A thought is blossoming in some corner of my mind – something unexpected and yet expected, something obvious but profound.

"*Disconnected*," I repeat, waiting for it to reveal itself.

"Take my job," Tom says. "It's all about turning one currency into another, about swapping one kind of money to another kind. I mean, what's the point?"

"What's the point of anything," I say. "I mean, if you..."

"That's not true," Tom says. "I mean, if you're growing food, or building furniture for people to sit on, or, I don't know, healing people..."

The thought is bursting out now, all over the shop. Realisation is rushing – like a tidal wave – into my mind. A deep, powerful swell of overdue comprehension about who Tom is, about what he needs, and above all, about why the whole episode with Dante happened.

"Is that why Dante was so..." I say, propping myself up on one elbow.

Tom nods and frowns. "Dante? Oh... I suppose so," he says. "I mean, I didn't see Dante for what he was really... I saw him as... Oh I don't know..."

"A symbol?" I say.

Tom nods. "Maybe," he says. "A symbol of a better way of living." He sighs. "Certainly got that one wrong, didn't I."

I nod and lick my lips as I take this in. Realising that in a couple of seconds I have understood, and that in understanding I have forgiven, I start to smile.

"Dante was your all-in-one solution," I say.

Tom snorts. "Yeah, well, I have an all-in-one solution for Dante," he says. "*Death*."

I frown at Tom's sudden bitterness. It's not that I don't understand, it's just that it isn't like him. "That's maybe a bit extreme," I say. "But I know what you mean."

Tom looks at me seriously. "He should die for what he did," he says quietly. "He would have killed us, you know."

I shrug. "Yeah, well, lets not get into a whole debate about the death penalty, eh?"

Tom frowns at me. "Don't *you* think he should die? Don't you think the world needs to be protected from madmen like him?"

I roll my eyes. "The trouble with the death penalty – and you know it – is that no system, no government, is ever trustworthy enough to be allowed to take those decis…"

"But I know, *we* know," Tom says. "If I had the chance to kill him, don't you think I should?"

"Tom," I say. "Maybe. I don't know. Probably not. I mean, he didn't actually kill anyone. But it's immaterial; because you don't have the chance, do you… If you really wanted to do something, then you know what I think… that you should go to the police."

Tom shakes his head. "I can't, I couldn't… I couldn't get involved, and who would believe me. And he'd have Paolo on his side… We talked about this already."

I nod. "Well we never did really," I point out. "Look… I don't know why we're talking about it now. That's not the point I was making at all."

Tom swallows hard and nods. "My fault," he says. "Sorry, carry on."

I have to think for a moment to remember where I was. "What I was saying… suggesting…" I say eventually. "Is that Dante wasn't just a symbol, he was a practical means too, a way to change your life."

Tom nods. "An escape route," he says. "And a guru too."

I nod. "Oh Tom," I say, laying my head on his chest. "I'm so sorry."

It's a strange thing to say. And what I mean, that I'm sorry it didn't work out with Dante, that Dante let him down so badly, is an even stranger thing to think. But it's true, and it's heartfelt. I can see how Dante came to represent salvation for Tom. I can see why he attached so forcefully, so madly to the wholesome living philosopher guru. And I am only now grasping just how badly that fall from grace has hurt him.

"No," Tom says, stroking my hair. "*I'm* sorry."

For some reason, something to do with the tenderness I'm feeling towards him, I can feel an erection stirring. It seems… what would Tom say? *Inappropriate.*

"It was a mirage," Tom says.

"Dante?"

"The whole package," Tom says.

"In Dante's case," I say. "Well, it was worse than a mirage. It was a lie. But people *do* live like that. There *are* people who live quiet, ecologically responsible lives. They're just not Dante."

Tom breathes out heavily and rubs a hand across his face.

"You could build a life like that," I say. "If you wanted."

Tom shakes his head making his chest vibrate. "I couldn't," he says. "That's the whole thing. That's why I was looking for someone else to do it for me. Someone who had already done it."

I click my tongue, and move back next to him so that I can enlace him in my arms. "Oh babe," I say.

"I'm really lost right now," he says, his voice weak. "And still angry too... knowing that he's still there, that he's just carrying on his..." Tom looks at my frown and sighs. "I'm sorry..." he says. "I am lost though... I feel like I'm floating, like I'm disconnected from everything. Like I don't know where I'm going."

"But that's okay," I say. "I mean, we all feel like that sometimes. That's what relationships are for."

"Are they?" Tom says with mock humour. "I always wondered."

I pull away just enough to look into his eyes. "Sure," I say. "They're so that when one person's lost, the other knows the way. You just have to take it in turns."

Good Thing Bad Thing

I watch Tom's buttocks moving up and down beneath his beige cotton shorts as he weaves along the path before me. They are fleshier than before – with the weight he has put on – but they are actually more sensual, more inviting because of it.

He turns his head half towards me and says, "Where do you think this path actually goes? I mean, why would anyone go this way?"

I shrug and weave around a bush; it's covered in tiny purple flowers. "Maybe just tourists," I say. "Hill-walkers and the like."

To our right the Alps begin in earnest, thrusting up from the flat of the land into jagged snow-capped points unworn by millions of years of weather. To the left the valley sweeps to the north, green and deep and lush with an almost unbelievably turquoise river along the middle.

Our own path weaves along from the tiny hamlet we're staying in to an outcrop of grey, marble-like rock in the distance, weaving its way up and along the ridge of this, the largest of the foothills or the smallest of the southern Alps, I'm not sure which.

The air is cold, the sky a stunning deep blue; the sun, piercing through the thin air, pricks my arms as though they were covered with drying salt.

We have only walked ten minutes from the *gite*, but as far as the eye can see – and that's a long, long way – there is no sign of life at all, no indicator of human society apart from this thin dusty path worn through the scrub by the constant flow of people wanting, for no apparent reason, to walk to the same point we are now approaching.

At the tip of the outcrop we see that the path actually continues, weaving down the side of the rock face and on up, way into the distant mountains.

"When you said the Alps," Tom tells me, pausing and pulling a bottle of water from his backpack, "I thought you meant, like, hills... I didn't realise there were proper mountains like this around here."

He hands me the bottle of water and I take a mouthful before replying. "Nope, those are the real thing," I say. "What now? Onward and downward?"

Tom looks to his left and nods towards a lone gnarled plane tree. "Shall we sit in the shade a bit first? I know we haven't gone far, but..."

I shrug and head past him to the shade. "It's not a race," I say.

The leaves shift as the branches oscillate in the gentle breeze. We lie on our backs watching the light filtering through the almost fluorescent green of the leaves, at the turquoise sky peeping through the gaps.

"Have you noticed how good the air smells?" Tom asks.

I hadn't, but I do now. I breathe in deeply and mull over the mixture – burnt earth, a cold, metallic mountain smell, floral hints from the wild lavender... "Yeah, it's amazing," I say. "And the noise of the insects. They sound like a squadron of B-52's."

Tom cocks his head and listens and then turns and points at a tiny tree behind us. "It's bees in those white flowers," he says. "Amazing."

"Elderflower I think," I say. "My dad used to make wine out of it."

"Elderflower wine?" Tom says.

I nod and wrinkle my nose. "Tasted like cat's piss... Not that I ever tasted cat's piss of course."

Tom frowns. "So why did he make it?"

I shrug. "Dunno. People just did. The war generation... well, they made wine out of anything... out of *everything* in fact."

Tom breathes in deeply. "It makes you want to breathe more... This air, it sort of makes you conscious of the pleasure of breathing."

A fly is buzzing around Tom's chin. He swipes it away repeatedly. "They never show the bugs," Tom says. "In films, I mean."

I smile.

"It's always idyllic picnics and stuff. Never people picking wasps from the chutney."

I grin. "I think it is pretty idyllic," I say, flicking an ant from my leg. "Despite all the beasts."

Tom reaches over and grasps my hand. "Me too," he says. "It's stunning. Really."

We lie for a moment watching the patterns formed by the leaves. Tom sighs heavily.

"Happy sigh or unhappy sigh?" I ask.

Tom snorts. "Ah! The master of the complex sigh!" he says mockingly.

I raise an eyebrow and roll my head towards him. "So?" I prompt.

Tom shrugs. "A mixture I suppose," he says. "Sort of a happy/sad sigh."

I frown, so he continues, "It's just that this is so perfect, and that makes me think about going back, and going back makes me think what a difficult year it's been, and that kind of makes me sad."

"The bitter-sweet edge of joy," I say. "The fact that nothing ever lasts."

Tom swipes at the fly again and nods. "Yeah," he says. "Something like that." He thinks for a moment and then says, "In the same way, sadness should make you happy really."

I frown at him.

"I mean, if when you were sad you thought about the fact that it never lasts either... well it could work the other way around. Only I never seem to get sadness tinged with happiness..."

"You *are* feeling better though, aren't you?" I ask him gently. "I mean, you seem better."

Tom nods vaguely. "I think so," he says. "I still feel a bit... Well, a bit vague really. And sometimes that worries me; because it feels like that curtain..." He clears his throat. "...that curtain of disconnectedness is coming back again. And that scares me. But it actually doesn't. It hasn't been anywhere near as bad really. Not since I stopped the Prozac. Ironically."

I nod. "Good," I say. "Jumping through coffee tables at 4 AM was getting scary."

"I still have the scar," Tom says, lifting his t-shirt and showing me his side. "Anyway... it's still hard," Tom says. "In a way. I mean these holidays help..."

I frown at him.

"Oh, don't get me wrong... this is lovely. It *really* helps. But it almost makes going back worse."

I nod and sigh. "Well, you really need to think about quitting that job then," I say. "I mean, you've never liked it."

Tom nods. "I know," he says. "But it's not that simple. I mean, it's a family business. You can't just walk out without warning."

I shrug. "You could give notice though," I say. "If you're really unhappy."

Tom picks a blade of grass and chews it and I copy him and do the same. It tastes bitter with chlorophyll.

"Maybe later in the year," Tom says. "I kind of owe my uncle a favour."

"What for?" I say.

Tom licks his lips, but then looks away. "Oh, nothing really, just family stuff. You know how it is."

I roll my head back and look up through the leaves again. The flickering light tires my eyes, so I close them and after a few minutes I am hovering on the edge of sleep – still aware of the insects buzzing, of Tom beside me, but also starting to drift and dream. It feels gorgeous.

"Have you noticed how nice people are up here?" Tom says. His voice suddenly seems very loud.

I force my eyes open. "Yeah, everyone's been really sweet," I say.

"That cook, in the restaurant last night, in, where was that place?"

"Guillaumes?"

"Nah, not the town. What was the restaurant called?"

I shrug. "*Le Provençal* or something," I say.

"The way the cook pulled up a chair and just, you know, joined us..." Tom says. "I can't remember the last time anyone took the time to do that."

"I think he was intrigued by our marital arrangements," I say. "You know how he kept asking which of us was married to Jenny. Which of us was Sarah's dad. I think he thought we were some sort of *ménage a trois.*"

Tom giggles. "Yeah. I guess. But he still wasn't rushing home was he. I mean, in England, he'd be rushing home after work to watch TV, *Big Brother* or something... He was more interested in us, in *our* lives."

I shake my head. "I guess," I say. "But then French TV *is* shockingly bad."

"I wish there was no TV at all," Tom says.

"Says the man who just bought a sixty-four inch widescreen," I laugh.

"It's thirty-two," Tom says. "But if *everyone* didn't have TV, well, you wouldn't *get* bored would you. Because everyone would be looking for things to do." Tom brushes away another fly, or it could be the same fly. "If everyone agreed to give up telly at the same time, I'd do it tomorrow."

I nod. "Yeah," I say. "Me too."

"Will you go away!" he says exasperatedly swatting at the fly again.

"The great outdoors," I say.

Tom jumps to his feet and reaches out to help me up. "Let's go back and have lunch," he says. "I'm starving."

"The great adventurer," I laugh.

Tom frowns.

"Ten minutes out and ten minutes back," I say.

Tom grins and pulls me to my feet. "Hey, put lunch inside me and this afternoon this baby will go as far as you want," he says.

"As far as I want," I say provocatively raising an eyebrow. "Sounds good."

As we round the final bend – where the path joins the circular track that rings the tiny hillock that is Chateaneuf d'Entraunes, Sarah comes into view.

"Mark!" she shouts starting to run wobblingly towards us. She calls both Tom and myself "Mark" for the moment. Jenny says it's because of the goatees. Jenny trots into view a few feet behind, grinning.

"Weird seeing her so grown up already," Tom says. "I know it's a cliché, but it does seem to happen so fast."

"Hello boys," Jenny says breathlessly.

"She running you ragged?" I laugh.

"Oh she's having a whale of a time, aren't you... It's great because there's no cars."

Sarah points vaguely the way she came and says, quite clearly, "Shit!"

"Sheep," Jenny instantly translates. "And they're goats, but... well..." She shrugs. "Anyway, I'm glad to see you two... I was wondering what to do about lunch."

Tom sweeps Sarah up and onto his shoulders and starts to jog off along the track. "Show me where the shit is," he says.

"Have a good walk?" Jenny asks me, linking her arm through mine.

I snort. "We didn't get far," I say. "The great adventurer there sat down under the first tree. It was nice though."

"Tom seems better," Jenny says. "He seems more human since he got here."

I nod, "Yeah, the country is definitely his thing."

"Oh," Jenny says, glancing surreptitiously up the path and pulling a folded newspaper page from her pocket. "I took this... from your *Sunday Times*."

She hands me the folded paper. I frown and shake it open. "What is it?" I ask.

"I thought..." Jenny starts, but Tom has turned and is looking back at us. "Hey look..." he says, but then his eyes drop to the page in my hand, and his interest roused he starts to walk back towards us. Sarah, frustrated on his shoulders strains and points the other way. "Shit!" she says. "Shit!"

Jenny tuts and snatches the page back from me. "God you're hopeless," she says, quickly re-folding the page and stuffing it into her pocket.

"What is it?" Tom asks, now back with us.

I shrug. "I don't... I didn't..."

"It's nothing," Jenny says. "It's secret."

Tom frowns. "Show me," he says.

Jenny shakes her head and walks on. "It's not happening," she says. "So forget it."

Tom looks at me worriedly and I shrug. "Dunno..." I tell him.

"Look," Jenny says pointing down the hill.

About thirty feet below a natural terrace has been turned into a vegetable garden. The woman from the *gite* is watering a row of freshly planted vegetables.

146

"Is that Chantal from the *gite*?" Tom asks.

"Yeah," Jenny says. "Poor bitch."

As if she has heard us – which is impossible – Chantal straightens, looks up at us, presses one hand into the small of her back and waves with the other. We wave back.

"Why do you say that?" Tom asks. "I think they have a wonderful life up here."

"Hard though," I say.

"Not really," Tom says. "Not compared with traffic jams and public transport. I think she's really lucky."

"Says the man who walks ten yards and then needs to sit under a tree," I point out.

Tom laughs. "You have me all wrong," he says. "I love gardening."

Jenny snorts. "When did you ever garden?"

"I helped my dad on the allotment all the time," Tom says.

"Whatever," Jenny says with a wave of the hand. "But so far I've seen her make beds, serve us breakfast with a baby under her arm, cook dinner and now she's watering vegetables."

"With a watering can," I say. "I mean, she could at least treat herself to a hose pipe."

"And where's the husband?" Jenny points out. "So I say, poor exploited bitch!"

"I wonder if that's our lunch," Tom says, ignoring Jenny's cynicism.

"I hope not," I laugh. "She's just planted it. Unless you're counting on having lunch in September."

Tom laughs. "In the basket, *idiot!*"

Jenny shakes her head. "It's not," she says, reaching out for Sarah's hand. "We didn't book lunch, remember? We said we were going to that other town for lunch. The one after Guillaumes."

"Valberg," I say.

Tom pulls a face. "Really? Oh... Well, come on," he says, suddenly spurting forward. "Let's get going! I'm bloody starving."

U nlike every other day, Tom won't get up for breakfast. Unlike every other day Tom *needs* to get up – he has a plane to catch at lunchtime. When I reach the dining room Jenny and Sarah are already settled at our favourite table – the one with the stunning view over the Alps.

Jenny is saying, "*Don't!*" and pulling Sarah's finger from the sugar bowl. She looks up at the sound of the door closing. "Morning sleepyhead," she says. "I was just thinking about waking you two up."

I finish my yawn and pull up a chair.

"Help yourself," Jenny says, rotating the coffee pot so that the handle is facing me. "There's plenty."

I ruffle Sarah's hair affectionately, but she pulls away in irritation. I pour myself a cup of the thick black liquid. "The croissants any better today?" I ask Jenny who has taken to dipping hers, French style, into her coffee.

"Nope," she says. "The only horrible croissants in France."

"I think they're those long life ones," I say. "But then, I suppose there isn't any kind of bakery here."

"They're okay if you dunk them," Jenny says.

I wrinkle my nose and start to smother mine with butter.

"Where's Tom?" Jenny asks, pulling a lump off her croissant and putting it on Sarah's plate to replace the one she has just thrown on the floor. "Packing?"

I shake my head. "He pulled a pillow over his head and told me to fuck off," I say. "Me thinks the man doesn't want to go home."

Chantal pushes backwards through the door from the kitchen carrying a tray containing a fresh pot of coffee and more dodgy croissants.

"Bonjour," she says brightly, sliding the tray onto the edge of the table.

I thank her and move things around on the table so that everything fits, but today Chantal – who usually seems to be rushed off her feet – lingers.

"*Tout le monde est parti?*" Jenny says slowly. Her accent makes me giggle. She sounds like Jane Birkin.

"Yes," Chantal replies, her accent as strong as Jenny's. "Everyone go – only you."

I smile at her and shrug.

"And today you leave too!" she says.

Jenny nods. "But I bet you'll be glad," she says. "You seem very busy..."

Chantal nods and Jenny frowns, then says, carefully, *"Trop de travail!"*

Chantal nods again. "Yes it is very 'ard." She looks at me solemly and then lapses into French. *"Depuis que Jean est parti..."*

When she has gone, and the kitchen door has swung closed behind her, Jenny looks at me and nods seriously. "Did she just say what I think she said?"

I nod. "Don't tell Tom," I say.

S arah points and says, "Sheep!"
"Hey she said it right!" I remark.
Jenny, who is driving says, "Yes doll, that's right. *Sheep*."
"Goats," Tom says glumly. "They're *goats*."

Jenny glances back at us, then returns her regard to the road and powers the VW out of the bend. "There aren't any goats in her animal book," she says. "Don't be so mean."

I try to take Tom's hand but he pulls away. "What's up with you?" I say, sighing and watching from his side window as Chateauneuf D'Entraunes disappears behind a hill.

"I can't believe you didn't save me a croissant," he says. "You know how starving I am in the morning."

"I can't believe you didn't get up for breakfast," I retort.

Jenny glances at us in her rear-view mirror and I catch her eye momentarily. "We can stop in Guillaumes," she says. "You can go to the bakery and get as many croissants as you like Tom."

Tom raises an eyebrow. "See," he says. "*Jenny* cares."

I drop my mouth in fake outrage. "That's so unfair," I say.

Tom turns away, and I watch what he's watching – the green valley surrounding the riverbed, a farmhouse, a donkey in a field...

"Don't you feel sad?" Tom asks. "Having to leave all this behind. I mean, doesn't it get to you?"

"It was nice," I say. "But holidays end."

"Tell him," Jenny says. "Don't be mean."

Tom turns his frown upon me. "Tell me what?" he says.

I shrug. "Nah," I say. "Sorry, it's a secret."

Tom turns silently back to watching the countryside slip by.

I glance at the front and see Jenny looking at me again.

"He's being horrible," I say. "Never reward bad behaviour."

Jenny shrugs. "It might cheer him up," she says, a note of sarcasm in her voice.

Tom turns back to face me again. He's intrigued now. "What?" he says.

I shrug.

"I'll be good," Tom laughs, starting to smile. "Honest."

"Oh it's nothing really," I say. "I was thinking, maybe it might be nice to do something like that together one day."

Tom's swivels slowly around in his seat. "Like what?" he says.

I suppress a grin. "Like run a *gite*, or a bed and breakfast or something."

Tom stares at me, solid as a rock. He looks puzzled.

I smile at him and he snorts and then slips into the widest, sweetest grin I have ever seen. "You're not joking?" he says.

I shrug. "We're both sick of our jobs... I mean, why not?"

Tom takes my hand. "You *are* serious right?" he says again, his eyes now visibly watering. "Because if you're winding me up... I'd be heartbroken I think."

"Well we have to think about it properly Tom. It would take lots of planning, and it'd be hard work."

Tom smiles. "The man from Del Monte, he say, *Yes*. No hesitation."

I nod. "Well, we still need to think about it all... It really isn't an easy option. Not financially, not physically. Let's look around and think about it..."

At the airport Tom slides the door open and steps onto the pavement. He grins broadly. "I'll call you when I get in," he says. "I'm... well, I'm really excited actually."

I kiss him goodbye. "Well, try and stay calm," I say. "It ain't gonna happen overnight. And you might wake up in a cold sweat at 3 AM and decide that it's not what you want at all."

"Or you might," he says.

I shrug. "I'm ready for an adventure too," I say. "It's fun just thinking about it anyway."

Tom glances at his watch. "I guess I have to go," he says.

I nod and reach for the door.

Tom leans through Jenny's window and kisses her on the cheek, then glances at Sarah and pouts. "Tell the little one I said goodbye," he says.

Jenny grins, gives a little wave and then accelerates away.

"The little one won't notice he's gone," she says dryly. "The little one thinks you are two manifestations of the same person."

I wave to Tom from the rear window and then settle back in my seat for the final drive home. "Well, that cheered him up," I say.

Jenny nods. "I can't believe you didn't tell him though, about the *gite*, I mean," she says.

I shrug. "I suppose I don't want to get his hopes too high just yet," I say. "There's plenty that could go wrong," I point out. "I mean, she might not sell the place after all, her husband could come back, she might get an estimate and double the price..."

"I suppose so," Jenny says vacantly, indicating and pulling sharply into the traffic on the Promenade des Anglais.

"It was enough to send him back happy anyway..." I say. "And if Chantal does call me and confirm the sale price, well, that'll be a fresh round of good news. The way I see it, Tom needs as much good news as he can get."

"Oh!" Jenny exclaims. "I nearly forgot." She pulls a folded sheet of paper and proffers it behind her back.

"Oh yeah," I say, reaching for it. "The newspaper mystery."

"I thought it best that Tom not see that," she says. "Well, not unless you think he should anyway."

"What is it?" I ask as I unfold the double-page sheet.

Jenny shrugs. "Read it," she says. "And no shouting or screaming please, Sarah's asleep."

I scan the various articles on the page but nothing catches my eye. Jenny glances back at me and makes a tutting sound. "Other side," she says.

New Twist In Italian Murder Mystery

Pignone, Italy – Terrorised inhabitants of a sleepy town, more used to lost tourists than bloody murder mysteries, awoke today to discover that yet another murder has been committed on their patch.

Much of Italy's media visited the town in April following the grisly discovery – following a series of anonymous tip-offs – of two young men's bodies buried at a local farm. Public interest was fed by interviews with locals and speculation over the identity of the murderer but when investigations failed to throw up any useful leads, interest waned and the town was left to come to terms with the unsettling knowledge that the perpetrator remained at large.

The sensational events of the last week have thrown Pignone back under the full glare of the media spotlights with a fresh batch of anonymous calls to Police resulting in the discovery of a third body on Sunday.

Gruesome Details Leaked To Press

Details of the gruesome deaths were leaked to the press before the police had even begun their investigations, prompting accusations of incompetence.

The sensationalist *Chi magazine* voiced speculation that the manner of the deaths – prolonged beatings and slashed throats – suggested the involvement of satanic cults, whilst the more serious *La Repubblica* pointed the finger soberly at the Mafia even naming specifically the Corleone clan.

With the revelation that the latest victim was not just anyone, but the son of wealthy French business mogul Jean-Claude Robero, the scandal could only deepen, whilst controversy raged over the refusal of local Police to question Dante Migliore, the owner of the farm where the bodies were discovered. The Police Nationale placed Migliore beyond suspicion calling him, "a well respected member of the local community."

But as dawn broke on Monday, Migliore was found dead on the steps of the local Police station, the cause of death a single bullet wound to the head.

Accusations once again have centred on Mafia involvement, even bringing denials from the Corleone clan – unprecedented from a family that traditionally shuns the media. A spokesman told Rai Uno, 'First we are accused of protecting this Migliore character, and then we are accused of murdering him. It's absurd....'

continued on page 72.

I frown and flip the piece of paper. "Where's the rest?" I say.

Jenny shrugs. "It just went on about that Mafia family, the Correones or whatever..."

"Wow," I say. "He's dead."

"Yeah... I wasn't sure if it was good news or if it was better not to tell Tom, better he doesn't think about Dante at the moment..."

I shiver involuntarily.

"Mark?" Jenny says.

I swallow hard.

Jenny touches my thigh. "Mark, what's wrong?" she says.

I shake my head. "I don't know," I say. "I really don't know."

I stare at the newspaper clipping. Paloma rubs frantically around and between my legs. She's begging for food, not because she needs food – a neighbour dropped by this morning – but because feeding her is what I have to do when I get home. It's how she knows I care.

I put the page down on the coffee table and replace one batch of food with another. Paloma purrs ecstatically. Then I grab a glass of water and sit and stare at the page again, waiting for the free-association filing system that is my brain to do its thing and come up with some ideas.

"Dante is dead..." I run that thought through my mind. Murdered and dumped on the steps of a police station.

I wrinkle my nose. I wouldn't wish a death sentence on anyone, but I can't say I'm sad about it either. I remember discussing exactly that with Tom. He won't be sad either. *Au contraire.*

I wonder if he already knows. The page comes from Tom's newspaper after all, and it's hard to imagine he spent two hours in the airport and then an hour and a half on a plane *without* reading it. Could he really have missed it? And if not then why didn't he tell me?

Yes, Tom would be thrilled at Dante's death. It would be the first thing he would tell me. If he knew. And if he wasn't hiding something.

I shiver, for there it is, the thought I have been trying to avoid facing. In fact who would want Dante dead *more* than Tom? Well, any of the relatives of the deceased I guess. And maybe it *was* the Mafia... The Corleone family... But why?

I huff, and drop the clipping again and start to stroke Paloma who has reappeared at my side. I imagine men in dark suits slipping in, screwing on a silencer, and positioning the gun against Dante's head.

In my mind's eye, the killers are stocky men in dark suits. Men with bad skin, shiny shoes and Bluetooth earpieces. Men like the thugs at Tom's father's funeral. Like the lurking pedestrian outside Tom's flat.

I shudder again. Of course I'm being ridiculous. I didn't even see the guy outside Tom's flat. But all the same... And Tom's uncle, Tom's work colleagues. Why do they all look so dodgy. Why does the Gambino family look so shady? Gambino. It even *sounds* like a Mafia.

Mysterious foreign exchange operations, a new Mercedes... The more I think about it, the worse it gets.

I close my eyes and raise my fingers to support my temples. This is out of hand... I can't possibly be dating a Mafia son... *or can I?* I feel guilty for even imagining the possibility.

I walk through to the kitchen and switch on the kettle and stand, a little numb, and watch it boil. *A watched kettle never boils*, I think obtusely. *Where there's smoke there's fire.*

I check my watch. Another hour and a half before Tom gets home.

The phone rings a little earlier than I expected – I am in the shower. I even imagined that this would happen when I turned on the tap. I skid across the bathroom floor to the bedroom and swipe the phone from the base.

"Hiya," I say. "I was in the shower."

"Oh, shall I call b..."

"No it's fine," I interrupt.

"Okay, well... I'm home," Tom says. His voice is distant, strained.

"Okay, well, *good*," I say. "It all arrived on time then, the flight and stuff..."

"Yeah," Tom says. "And I opened my post."

I frown. "Yeah?"

"*Yeah*," Tom says.

I pull a face at Tom's cagey replies. "Anything interesting?"

There's a pause. Tom coughs. "Yeah," he says. "I suppose so."

I shiver and start to towel myself off. "You suppose so?" I repeat.

"Yeah," Tom says slowly. "I take it there's something you want to tell me."

I sit on the edge of the bed, my brow furrowed. "Is there?" I say. "I thought maybe *you* had something you wanted to tell *me*."

Tom clicks his tongue. "Look, can we stop playing games here?" he says. "I'm tired, I don't know what you're up to and frankly, it's irritating the fuck out of me."

"I'm not playing anything Tom," I say. "I don't know what you mean."

"Okay, let's start with why you posted this?"

"Posted what?"

"The *page*! It arrived. Perfect timing," he says, his tone rich with sarcasm. "Well done."

"Tom, I…"

"So tell me."

"I don't know what you're…"

"Mark, the page from my newspaper. You took it."

"From the *Times*? About Dante?"

"Bingo! From the *Times*. About Dante," Tom spits.

"So you *do* you know about that… Yes, Jenny took it. She gave it to me."

"Well of course I know about it… That's the point, isn't it?"

There's a long pause.

"I'm sorry Tom," I say. "This conversation makes no sense to me. Can we rewind and just start again?"

"Jesus Mark!" Tom says. "You're really starting to piss me off. Why the fuck did you do that? Answer me. Are you trying to freak me out? Because if so, well, it's worked."

"I… Look Tom," I say. "I don't know what I'm supposed to have done. Honestly."

"You stole the page from my newspaper,"

"Jenny did. She thought it might upset you," I say. "That's all."

"Whoever stole it, I don't really care. What I want to know is why you posted it here."

I frown and shake my head as I try and work this out. "I… didn't," I tell him. "I mean, I have it here. I'm holding it. Jenny gave it to me in the van, after we dropped you off."

"Well I have it too," Tom says. "And it looks like your handwriting on the envelope."

"Well it isn't babe," I say.

"Look if this is some kind of a…"

"Tom," I interrupt. "Listen to me. I'm telling you the truth. Jenny saw the article. She hid it – so it wouldn't upset you – and then she gave it to me this evening. End of story."

"Read it to me," Tom says.

"What do you mean, *read* it to you?"

"Read it! If you have it."

"Tom, this is ridiculous."

"Read it. Please."

"New twist in Italian murder mystery," I say, my voice flat with restrained anger. "Terrorised inhabitants of a sleepy town, more used to lost tourists ..."

"Okay. Read the other side," Tom says.

"Why?"

"Please," Tom says.

I flip the page and shake my head. "Jesus Tom!" I say. "Which bit? Tech stocks crumble as Nasdaq falters? Or hottest summer for fifty years..."

"Okay, Okay," Tom says. "It's not a photocopy."

I take a deep breath and wait angrily for Tom to continue. "Sorry," he says eventually. "But something weird is going on..."

"Yeah," I say. "Well..."

"I tried to read my newspaper on the plane, and there were pages missing. And then when I got home they were posted through the letterbox."

"Pages?" I say. "Did you say pages?"

"Yeah, well, it's in two parts," Tom says. "The main bit and the end of the article is on like page seventy or something."

"I haven't seen that bit," I say. "It must still be in your newspaper."

I hear Tom rustling the pages of the newspaper. Then Tom says, "Okay, so I have two page seventy-two's... My own, and the one you... the one someone else sent. So I believe you."

"Well thanks," I say.

We sit in silence for a moment, and then Tom says, "So he's dead."

I nod silently, and then say, "Yeah."

"I can't say I'm sad."

I shake my head. "No," I say.

"But who could know that *I'd* be interested?" Tom says. "I mean, why send it to me?"

"Maybe whoever killed him," I venture.

"But how would they know. How would they have my address for fuck's sake?"

"Where was the letter posted Tom? I mean, where's the postmark?"

"In France somewhere..." Tom says. "That's why I thought... Oh, no, hang on. Sorry, it was posted in Italy actually – *Milan*. I was so angry I didn't look properly..."

"Do you know anyone in Milan?" I ask.

Tom sighs. "No," he says. "Not really..."

"Not really?" I repeat.

"Well, we have an office there. But I don't know them or anything."

"So, did you ever tell anyone about Dante?" I ask. "Anyone at work?"

"No," Tom says. "Not really..."

"Again, those words... What do you mean, *not really*?"

"I might have mentioned it vaguely... in an argument about the death penalty. But I definitely didn't give any specifics. Not enough to know what happened, or who, or where..."

"Humm... Are you really sure Tom, because..."

I let him think about it. After a minute or so, he says. "No, definitely not. I'm not that proud of it all, really, if you know what I mean."

"And you never told your uncle," I say.

"Mark, this is ridiculous," Tom says. "My uncle may be a bit of a roughneck, but he doesn't go about executing people."

"*No*," I say.

"He doesn't!" Tom says.

"Okay, okay!" I say. "But someone does."

"Yeah."

We sit in silence for another minute or so. I'm racking my brain for an explanation. Tom is no doubt doing the same.

"And you?" he says. "Did *you* ever mention it to anyone?"

I sigh. "What? To any of the hit men I know?"

"Look Mark, I don't know, but somehow..."

"Well of course I didn't Tom," I say. "I mean Jenny knows."

"Yeah," Tom says. "Jenny."

"Oh come on," I say. "Anyway... Jenny hid the clipping from you. She wouldn't hide it from you *and* send it to you."

"No," Tom says.

I think for a moment then say, "I guess we still don't go to the police?"

Tom snorts. "You guess right. You did *read* the article right? Mafia connections, summary executions... a police cover up..."

"Right," I say.

I wait for Tom to reply but he says nothing, so eventually I prompt him. "You still there?"

"Yeah," he replies.

"What are you thinking?"

"Erm, I'm thinking that I'm scared," Tom says.

"Right," I say.

"I mean, someone knows about Dante, someone killed him. Someone thoughtfully sent me the newspaper article... It's... It's scaring me."

"Tom, your uncle. I mean, he does look rough," I say. "How much do you really know about him?"

"Mark!" Tom says angrily. "My uncle does *not* have people executed."

"Okay," I say. "I just... I'm just trying to understand."

"And he didn't know," Tom says. "How *could* he know?"

"No," I say. "You're right."

"Mark?" Tom says.

"Yeah?"

"I'm shitting myself here."

I nod. "I know Tom," I say. "Me too."

I have been at work for less than half an hour when my phone rings. "C'est Tom," the secretary announces.

His voice is brittle, his stress crackles palpably over the line. "Mark," he says. "Listen, something's happened."

"Hi... Yeah, what?" I stumble.

"I didn't sleep, so I phoned in sick," Tom tells me, his voice rising at the end of the phrase to let me know that there is more to come.

"Yeah?"

"And I got put through to Claude – my uncle."

"Right," I say.

Carol the secretary moves in front of me holding out a letter. She's doing it on purpose. She has worked out that Tom is a personal call and bringing some work to me at this very moment is her dumb-arse way of reproving me. I wave her away as I would an insect.

"And... shit these units are going so fast. I'm in a callbox you see. I didn't want to use my mobile. Just in case."

"So what did he say? Your uncle..."

"Well, I told him I have some personal problems and I need more time off, and he asked if it was something to do with the letter."

"The *letter*? How did *he* know about the letter?"

"Well exactly," Tom says.

"Shit Tom, I don't like this. What did you say?"

"Fuck, I only have six units left. I asked what letter... and he said, *The letter the Milan people sent you.*"

"Tom this is so dodgy. Maybe you *should* go to the police or something."

"I didn't want to hear any more. I thought I was going to throw up, so I pretended my battery was running out and I hung up. I need time to think... I'm, I'm afraid he's going to tell me something, something incriminating, something I'm better off, you know, *safer* not knowing."

I want time to think about all of this too. "This is really fucked up Tom," I tell him. "I knew there was something wrong with your family."

"Thanks," Tom laughs dryly. "Anyway, the point is, I booked a flight. Can you pick me up at sixteen-forty?"

"You're coming back? *Tonight?*"

"Yeah," Tom says. "I didn't sleep a wink in my place. Every time someone walked past I woke up... so I was thinking of booking a hotel, and then I thought... Shit Mark, I really have no units left."

"I'll be there," I say.

"Thanks, sixteen-forty, I..." The line goes dead.

I lower the receiver and stare dumbly at the phone for a moment. A huge lump has formed in my throat. I feel sick myself.

"So the letter was from the *Milan people*," I murmur to myself. I stare at the phone as if this might reveal some clue I have missed. I desperately want to call him back, but of course if his phone's switched off, and he isn't at work and he isn't at home either...

Carol reappears holding the letter. She frowns at me in concern. *"Ca va?"* she says. *"T'as l'air tout pale..."* You look really pale.

Action precedes thought. I shake my head. "A... A friend died," I tell her. "A very, *very* good friend." My quick thinking almost makes me want to smile but I'm stressed to snapping point and the result is a strange grimace, it probably looks quite mad.

Carol eyes widen. *"Vraiment?"* she says.

I stand and grab my jacket from the stand. Carol eyes me nervously.

I blink at her slowly. "An accident he says... I... I have to go home," I say. "Tell him... tell him I'm sorry," I add nodding towards the boss's door. "Tell him, I'll call."

Carol nods and helps me on with my jacket. *"Je suis vraiment désolée,"* she says. I'm so sorry...

As Chateauneuf D'Entraunes comes into view, Tom leans forward and shouts, "I can't believe we're back here already!"

I lift up my visor and lean back towards him, all the while keeping my eyes on the winding road. "I know," I shout back. "Weird!"

The road transforms into the final series of hairpin bends, winding back and forth up the hill. The air is cooler up here – it's late afternoon, and the engine of my bike is purring contentedly as I power out of the bends. *"So much more fun than in a car,"* I think.

I pull up on the gravel outside the *gite*, and Tom climbs off, then I park the bike on the side-stand and pull off my crash helmet. The motor makes metallic twanging noises as it cools.

"Wow, that was great," Tom says. "I always feel so... I don't know. So free I suppose. It's like flying somehow."

I grin. "I was just thinking how much more fun it was too."

"And the smells... every town, every field has its own smell, and on the bike... well, it's great..." Tom's voice fades; he nods behind me and I turn to see Chantal standing in the doorway, the habitual sleeping baby under one arm.

"Déjà de retour!" she says. – Back so soon. *"Il va vraiment falloir que vous achetiez la maison!"*

I grimace and glance at Tom, but he hasn't understood or isn't listening. In fact he's swinging his crash helmet from side to side and staring at the Alps – the sun is just starting to set beyond the peaks. "Beautiful," he says.

"I nod. "And remote..." I say.

Tom sighs and turns to enter the house. "Yep, good thinking," he says.

"I thought it was as good a place as any for you to catch up on your sleep, and for us to try and work out what's going on," I say.

Tom nods and steps through the doorway, which Chantal is holding open for us. "Yeah..." he says, glancing sideways at Chantal and giving her a smile. "Let's leave that till tomorrow though, can we? My brain's numb with it all right now."

Chantal makes us omelettes and a simple green salad, followed by a single slice of *Tarte Tatin* she has left over from yesterday. The food here is pretty bad really, I could actually cook a much better meal, though possibly *not* with a child under one arm... Anyway, food isn't the reason that we're here.

We turn in immediately after dinner, returning to our old room. Tom pulls off his shoes and we sit, side by side and watch through the window – through the tiny glass pane set in these thick stone walls – as the sky turns blood-red – the mountains in stunning silhouette – then fades to purple.

"Imagine waking up to that view every morning," Tom says as the purple finally starts to fade to grey.

"Yeah," I say. "Imagine." *Imagine indeed.*

Over breakfast the next morning, I make Tom repeat, word for word, the exact conversation he had with his uncle. It pains him to do this – he's a great one for summing up – but my own brain works differently; my own brain thinks that there are clues in the words people choose, in the intonation even, that mean more than what is actually said.

But at the end of the walk-through, which Tom performs in a monotone voice and with a pained expression, there are no clues, there is no new information.

"None of it makes sense," I say. "I mean, none of the pieces fit. If your uncle had Dante killed and sent the letter then how did he know about you and Dante in the first place? And if he *didn't* send the letter then how did he know about *it* and how did whoever *did* send it get your address?"

"You like that theory, don't you," Tom splutters, his mouth full of long-life-croissant. "The Gambinos as Mafia murderers."

I shrug. "You take the piss, Tom. But until you come up with a better theory as to why he knew about the letter."

"Or you come up with a theory as to how he knew about Dante," Tom says.

I shrug. "Touché," I say.

Tom fingers his mobile.

"Is that bugging you?" I ask. "Do I need to take you into Guillaumes?"

Tom wrinkles his nose. "Yeah, not being contactable is part of the attraction I suppose… but I would like to at least know if I have messages."

I nod. "We can go now if you want…" I say.

Tom smiles weakly and drops the remaining half of his croissant on the plate. "We can get some proper breakfast too," he says.

Outside the bakery, Tom is sitting on a wall in the sunshine. I pull a croissant from the bag as I walk towards him and hand him the bag. "Here you go," I say. "They're still warm."

Tom takes it, puts his nose inside and breathes in deeply. "Wow," he says. "That's more like it… I was just thinking, how strange it must be to live somewhere where the sun shines all the time. Where you can plan what you're going to do every day because the weather does what it's supposed to do."

I nod. "Well, it's not sunny *every* day. This place is covered in snow in winter."

"I guess," Tom says. "But I bet at least when it snows, it *really* snows."

I sit down beside him and our thighs touch – we're both wearing three-quarter length shorts.

"So?" I say, nodding at the phone beside him. "Messages?"

Tom bites into his croissant, makes an *mmm* sound, and nods. "Five," he splutters.

"From your uncle?"

Tom nods, swallows, then replies, "Yeah. All five. I think he's really worried about me to tell the truth... I'm going to have to call him."

I flick a dead insect from my sweatshirt – a victim of our short ride down the hill. "I was thinking that too," I say. "It's the only way you're ever going to find anything out... We could stay here forever, but you still wouldn't know what was going on."

"Yeah," Tom says. "I know, I'll do it from there," he says, using his croissant to point at a phone booth across the square. "As soon as I've plucked up the courage. My batteries aren't that hot, and I'd hate to run out for real."

I sit on the wall and watch Tom's feet shuffle beneath the phone booth. After a while – it seems that this isn't going to be a quick call – my attention drifts and I study the life of the square.

The facades have all been repainted, the pavements recently replaced. It gives the town an artificial, stage-set kind of atmosphere. Doors open and people appear from the butchers, the bakers... I bet there *was* a candlestick maker here at some point. And then they wander slowly along to another door and disappear, sliding behind the reflections of the glass doors. It reminds me of some TV toy-town from my youth, *Trumpton* maybe.

After about half an hour the wall becomes uncomfortable and the sun a little too hot, so I cross the square to the shady side, and stand, then sit, with my back against a closed Ski-Shop.

From here I can see Tom who has also slid to the floor and is half crouching, half leaning against the stem of the phone booth – the cord of the telephone stretched taut. He has put his sunglasses on so I can't see his eyes. He is nodding soberly and occasionally scratching his knee.

My eyes wander around the square again, and I wonder how rural economies like this continue to function, what people actually *do* here. As far as I can see, this place continues to survive on the simple basis that the butcher buys beer in the bar, and the bar owner buys bread from the baker and the baker buys meat from the butcher. And *everyone* goes to the tobacconists.

A bead of sweat rolls down my arm, and I glance up at the sky wondering how hot it can get. It's the gentlest baby blue colour, dabbed with fleecy clouds, tiny and equally spaced throughout.

I fix the corner of a building and watch as the clouds drift behind it one by one. I yawn and notice that the pavement is starting to shimmer in the heat. I glance at the motorbike and realise that it is now in the sun – that the black plastic seat will be scalding, probably too hot to sit on. I stand to move it, but see Tom walking towards me across the square. He is shielding his eyes with one hand and flapping the bottom of his t-shirt with the other.

"So?" I say, as we meet each other on the pavement's edge.

Tom swallows and shrugs. "Can we go back?" he says. "I'm overheating here."

"Back to?"

"To the *gite*... I'll tell you all about it," he says. "But I need a moment to digest it all too."

I shrug. "Okay," I say doubtfully. "But everything's okay, right?"

Tom nods vaguely. "Yeah..." he says. "I think so."

We sit beneath 'our' tree. Tom hands me the bottle of water. The day is much hotter than when we were last here. It's so hot it seems even to have silenced the insects. I try and remember how long ago that was... It seems a world away, when in fact it's just a few days. "So tell me," I say, handing back the water. "I'm dying of information thirst here."

Tom swigs from the bottle – I watch his Adam's apple bob. Then he wipes his mouth on the back of his hand. "Okay," he says. "I haven't worked any of this out yet, but here's the deal."

I nod and shift towards him sitting cross legged. For some reason I think of the Buddha sitting beneath the tree of wisdom. "So enlighten me," I say with a smile.

"Right," Tom says. "So... It's hard to know where to start."

"The letter?"

"The letter..." Tom repeats. "Someone walked into our Milan office and asked if they knew how to get a message to Tom Gambino. Then they handed it over. End of story."

"Oh," I say frowning in disappointment. "Do we know who?"

Tom shakes his head. "Nope."

"Do we at least know how the Milan office got your address?"

Tom nods. "Yep. They phoned Claude. And that's the only reason *he* knew about the letter."

"He read it?"

Tom shakes his head. "I really don't think so. I can't imagine anyone daring to open it – not a letter to the boss's nephew, and they posted it directly to my home. And Claude *really* didn't seem to know anything about it. He asked me what it was and I had to bullshit him about it being from someone I fell out with ages ago, and how that was why I freaked about it."

I nod and sigh heavily. "Okay. So how did, *whoever*... How did they know the Milan office could even *get* a letter to you?"

Tom shrugs. "It's not so hard really. It's a forex office – it's called *Cambio Gambino*."

I wipe the sweat from my eyebrows. "Oh," I say again. "But surely you're not the only Tom Gambino in the world?"

Tom pulls a face. "Apparently we're reasonably well known around Milan. And there's not a lot of us left – it's a dwindling dynasty."

I nod knowingly. "And the Gambinos are known *for what exactly...?*" I say.

"Claude says we were quite big in the thirties... quite rich. But now, just for foreign exchange and banking stuff."

"Big in the thirties?" I say grinning and nodding at him suggestively.

Tom wrinkles his nose and half smiles. "I know what you mean... but... Oh, I don't know... He was really honest and quite sweet really... I even *asked* him if they were connected with the Mafia."

I bite my lip. "Was he upset?"

Tom shakes his head. "He just laughed like it was the silliest thing he ever heard. I felt quite bad actually."

"Did you ask him about that other family, the Corrleones?" I say.

Tom shakes his head. "How? Remember he hasn't read that newspaper article."

I nod and press the bottle of water against the side of my head. "So we still don't know who took the letter in... Paolo maybe?" I say.

Tom nods. "I was thinking that too. Remember what he was like when he saw my passport. He wouldn't have forgotten my name in a hurry."

"In which case Paolo shot Dante? Or got him shot?"

Tom shrugs. "Maybe he couldn't cover up for him anymore... Maybe he didn't want to be dragged down. It's all guesswork though isn't it."

"Maybe Paolo thought *you* were the source, the one sending all those anonymous tip-offs."

"I almost wish I had," Tom says. He lowers his gaze and then looks away at the grey mountains. "I didn't think of it though," he adds.

"I wonder who the other bodies are. They said there were three and one was a French businessman's son."

"There was nearly a fourth," Tom says with a serious nod. "The son of *another* wealthy businessman. I'm thinking more and more that maybe the reason it happened... happened to *me* I mean... Maybe the whole reason they held me in the first place was precisely because of my name, because of who my uncle is."

I nod thoughtfully. "You mean settling an old score or something?"

Tom shakes his head almost imperceptibly and then raises an eyebrow. "I was thinking more in terms of ransom possibilities."

I nod and think for a moment, then declare, "No, that doesn't make sense... *We* went *there*... You know? He didn't come and get us. *We* drove into Dante's..."

"Yeah," Tom says with a shrug. "Maybe he thought he got lucky. Maybe Dante couldn't believe his luck."

I sigh and shake my head.

"Anyway, the important thing is," Tom says, "that whoever *did* send the letter... well at least they don't have my address."

I lean across and run a hand up through his hair. "Yeah," I say. "That's one good thing. Though they *do* know where you work."

Tom sighs and then shrugs. "*Worked*," he says.

"Worked?" I repeat.

"Yeah," Tom says, pulling an, *oh-now-I've-gone-and-done-it* face. "I got the sack. Well, he asked me to leave."

"Really?"

Tom nods soberly. "Said I'm unreliable. And hysterical. And paranoid."

I bite my bottom lip and restrain a smirk. "I guess it must seem that way."

"It's *not* funny," Tom says. "Though I don't really blame him..."

I shrug. "You don't look too sad about it," I say.

"Well, we were talking about doing something else anyway," he says with a wink.

"Right," I say. "Hey, you know what though... I just thought... We didn't *quite* stumble into Dante's place."

Tom frowns at me.

"If I remember correctly, a friendly policeman took one look at your passport, told us the campsite was full, and sent us there."

Tom nods slowly. "Yeah..." he says. "Good old Paolo."

We sit in silence for a moment, then I say, "Maybe you should avoid Italy for a while."

Tom snorts. "Yeah," he says. "Maybe I should change my name."

I smile. "We could get married..." I laugh.

But Tom's smile fades, his voice shifts to a serious tone. "Can I ask you something?" he says.

"Yeah?" I say.

"How come you stayed with me? Through all that... I mean, I know I was... well... *awful* really."

I frown. "Where did *that* come from?"

Tom shrugs. "I was just wondering."

I shrug. "Ah, well... It was the money I expect," I laugh. "Plus, you were buying such lovely suits."

Tom sighs and shakes his head sadly. "I hate it when you do that," he says.

I take a deep breath, swallow hard and tip my head slightly to one side. "Sorry," I say. "I... I suppose I was intrigued," I say. "Even when I hated you, I wanted to understand why you did it. Maybe I loved... *love* you too much to just let go like that. I wanted to understand first..."

Tom nods. "And did you?" he asks. "Understand?"

I frown at him. "I think so Tom," I say. "More or less... When I came to see what Dante represented instead of what he actually was... well, the anger just fell away really."

Tom nods and stares at his feet. "Well, thanks," he says. "I'm glad you hung around."

I nod. "Me too," I say.

"I don't think I'll be wearing the suits so much," he says. ""I think I'm over that... Will that be a problem sir?"

I grin. "Nah," I say, stroking his cheek. "You look pretty good in biker gear too. We'll make do."

"Yeah... I suppose I have to get rid of the Mercedes," he says forlornly. "He's giving me three months pay, but I won't be able to keep the car."

"I wouldn't worry," I say. "I'm not sure that it's the ideal car anyway."

Tom wrinkles his nose. "I knew you never liked it," he says, pushing to his feet.

"I wasn't meaning that," I say, standing myself. "I was thinking you might be needing a different kind of car now, that's all."

Tom frowns and looks at me sideways.

"I was thinking, you might be needing a four-by-four. This place is under three feet of snow in the winter."

Tom frowns at me. "What? You want to come back here in winter?" he says.

I smile. "I was keeping it for a surprise," I say. "But, well... the place is up for sale."

Tom shakes his head. "What, *this* place? The *gite*?"

I nod. "Two-hundred thousand," I say. "Pretty cheap considering. Her husband walked and she's selling up."

Tom nods but says nothing. He doesn't look impressed, so – a little deflated – I shrug, and start to walk back along the track. Tom follows me silently.

As I reach the little stone hut, he touches my shoulder so I pause and turn to look at him.

"Mark, are you serious? Is it really for sale?"

I nod.

"And would you really think about doing it?"

I shrug. "I'm just saying that she's selling the place. And that together we could just about afford it. That's all."

Tom moves his mouth to speak and then closes it again.

"The gardening would be all yours," I say. "I hate gardening."

"Gardening..." Tom says in awe. "Wow, do we get the vegetable garden and everything?"

I nod. "The land goes all the way to... Well, to *here*," I say gesticulating at the stone hut behind me.

Tom spins to face the *gite*, then slowly turns, scanning the land between and finally looking back at the hut. "Wow!" he says. "That's huge!"

"Eleven hectares," I say. "It would take all of our money though. And the *gite* only makes about five thousand a year from guests at the moment, so it would be really tight."

"But we could grow our own veg," Tom says his voice now trembling with excitement. "And if the food wasn't so shit... you could really make this place work."

"*Who* could make it work?" I ask.

"I mean, *one* could..." Tom laughs.

"Yeah..." I say doubtfully. "Oh and Jenny said she might rent that studio apartment off us too," I say. "If we did move here."

Tom wide-eyes me and shakes his head. "Really? Would she really be up for it too?"

"She's up for renting a cheap apartment from us," I say. "I wouldn't count on her for much else..."

Tom pushes me back against the stone wall and kisses me. "I hope you're not joking," he laughs. "Because if you're winding me up, I'll have you."

I shrug. "So have me," I say, leaning forward and kissing him back. "But seriously, you have to think carefully about this... It's not a quick decision."

"I *have* thought carefully," Tom says, now pushing me sideways towards the doorway. "I'm a very quick thinker."

"But it won't be easy..." I say. "You do realise? It's a tough old life up here; three months snow..."

"Oh who wants easy," Tom says. "I've spent my entire life choosing the path of least resistance. Easy's boring."

I nod. "I know what you mean," I say.

"Plus," Tom laughs, manoeuvring me into the darkness of the hut, then reaching down into my shorts. "It never ends up being that easy, does it?"

I kiss him, and as he starts to unbutton my shorts I make a grab at his arm. "Tom," I say. "Not *here*..."

"Why?" he asks.

I shrug and relax my grip on his hand.

He kisses me on the lips and slides to his knees. The hut is dark and cold and as I feel his lips slip around my hardening dick, I glance out through the unglazed gap in the sidewall. The view is almost identical to that of our bedroom.

Tom pauses and I look down at him grinning at me. "If this place is going to be ours, then I think it's only proper that we..."

He laughs and licks the tip of my dick, swiping it with his tongue as if it were an ice cream. "Test the outbuildings," he says.

Epilogue

I walk through to the bedroom and lean in the doorway, watching Tom. He is staring at a load of suits he has piled up on the bed. He sighs deeply. "You're not having regrets are you?" I say, moving to his side and slipping an arm around his waist.

He smiles at me, wrinkles his nose and shakes his head. "Of course not," he says. "I was just calculating how much money I spent on all these stupid suits. It doesn't even seem worth packing them now."

I reach out and run the lapel of a grey silk number between finger and thumb. "I suppose you can't really wear them for gardening," I say. "Shame though."

"You think I should just dump them all?" Tom asks. "I could take them to a charity shop or something."

"I think you should keep a couple... At least keep the really nice ones," I say.

"For all the cocktail parties we'll be going to?" Tom laughs.

I shake my head and peck him on the cheek. "You could always wear them in the bedroom from time to time," I say. "I certainly wouldn't complain."

Tom grins broadly and bumps his hip against mine. "Okay, you choose then," he says.

"Just keep all the new ones," I say. "And that silk one! And get rid of any you haven't worn for a year."

Tom nods and sighs. "Okay," he says, folding the grey one and dropping it into an open removals box. "This one's in..." He reaches and pulls something from the pocket of the blue blazer beneath. "You saw that right?" he asks handing me the newspaper clipping.

"Yeah," I say, sitting on the edge of the bed and shaking the sheet open. "Well – the first half anyway."

The bed bounces as Tom sits down beside me.

"It's funny really," he says as I start to read. "I mean, if all that hadn't happened... I'm not sure we would even be here packing now. You know what I mean?"

I place a finger on the page so as not to lose my place and look up at him. "Good Thing Bad Thing?" I say.

Tom nods. "Yeah," he says meaningfully. "Good Thing Bad Thing." He pecks me on the cheek, and then stands to continue packing.

"Well, the *really* good thing here is that he's dead," I say.

"Yeah," Tom says. "Harsh, but true."

When I reach the bottom of the page, I unfold the second part and stare at the photograph – one of Dante's victims, and shiver. Then I read the caption and frown.

"Tom? Is this supposed to be Dante?" I ask. "Or someone he killed?"

Tom runs packing tape across the top of the box, adds it to the pile against the wall and returns to my side.

"Eh?" he says, bouncing back onto the bed.

"Look," I say, pointing at the caption.

"*Murdered – Migliore,*" Tom reads. He frowns at me. "No, that's not Dante. It must be one of the victims."

I shrug. "That's not what it *says*, Tom," I say. "*Murdered – Migliore*, that implies it's him... It implies that the picture is... was... Dante," I say. "Supposedly now dead."

"No way that's Dante," Tom says. "It's nothing like him."

I furrow my brow and slowly fold the page. "No," I say thoughtfully. "You're right. It's nothing like him at all."

Also Available From BIGfib Books

50 Reasons to Say "Goodbye"

A Novel
By Nick Alexander

Mark is looking for love in all the wrong places.
He always ignores the warning signs, preferring to dream, time and
again, that he has finally met the perfect lover until, one day…

Through fifty different adventures, Nick Alexander takes us on a tour
of modern gay society: bars, night-clubs, blind dates, Internet
dating… It's all here.
Funny and moving by turn, *50 Reasons to Say "Goodbye"*, is
ultimately a series of candidly vivid snapshots and a poignant
exploration of that long winding road; the universal search for love.

"Modern gay literature at its finest and most original."
– Axm Magazine, December 2004

*"A witty, polished collection of vignettes... Get this snappy little
number."*
– Tim Teeman, The Times

*"Nick Alexander invests Mark's story with such warmth... A
wonderful read – honest, moving, witty and really rather wise."* –
Paul Burston, Time Out

ISBN: 2-9524-8990-4
BIGfib Books.

For more information please visit:
www.BIGfib.com.

Sottopassaggio

A Novel
By Nick Alexander

I don't know how I ended up in Brighton. I'm in a permanent state of surprise about it.

Of course I know the events that took place, I remember the accident or rather I remember the last time Steve ever looked into my eyes before the grinding screeching wiped it all out. It all seems so unexpected, so far from how things were supposed to be...

Following the loss of his partner, Mark, the hero from the bestselling *50 Reasons to Say "Goodbye"*, tries to pick up the pieces and build a new life for himself in gay friendly Brighton.

Haunted by the death of his lover and a fading sense of self, Mark struggles to put the past behind him, exploring Brighton's high and low-life, falling in love with charming, but unavailable Tom, and hooking up with Jenny, a long lost girlfriend from a time when such a thing seemed possible. But Jenny has her own problems, and as all around are inexorably sucked into the violence of her life, destiny intervenes, weaving the past to the present, and the present to the future in ways no one could have imagined.

ISBN: 2-9524-8991-2
BIGfib Books.

Available from
www.BIGfib.com

The Dark Paintings

A Novel
By Hugh Fleetwood

Wealthy, depraved and hugely gifted, Luigi Teramo likes to think of himself as a cross between a pagan fertility god and an evil wizard.

Luigi has deliberately rejected his youthful talent for art in favour of making money, and of spending his fortune on young men and drugs. But he cannot bring himself to destroy the fruits of that rejected talent – his early paintings. And as the years pass, it starts to seem that those paintings possess a terrible power. A power that will cause Luigi's life to spin out of control, will destroy almost all who get close to him, and will end by involving him in blackmail, and murder…

The Dark Paintings is both a thriller and a black comedy – entertaining, shocking and profoundly disturbing.

"A tinge of the supernatural, a titillating whiff of the perverse, and – topping it off – a compelling miasma of creepiness…"
- Richard Labonte – Books To Watch Out For

ISBN: 2-9524-8995-5
BIGfib Books.

Available from
www.BIGfib.com

Printed in the United Kingdom
by Lightning Source UK Ltd.
114804UKS00001B/286-483